Stories by Contemporary Writers from Shanghai

# LABYRINTH OF THE PAST

T0097919

This book is edited and designed by the Editorial Committee of *Cultural China* series


Text by Zhang Yiwei
Translation by Cissy Zhao
Cover Image by Zhu Xinchang
Interior Design by Xue Wenqing
Cover Design by Wang Wei

Assistant Editor: Hou Weiting
Editor: Wu Yuezhou
Editorial Director: Zhang Yicong

Senior Consultants: Sun Yong, Wu Ying, Yang Xinci
Managing Director and Publisher: Wang Youbu

ISBN: 978-1-60220-245-0

Address any comments about *Labyrinth of the Past* to:

Better Link Press
99 Park Ave
New York, NY 10016
USA

or

Shanghai Press and Publishing Development Company
F 7 Donghu Road, Shanghai, China (200031)
Email: comments_betterlinkpress@hotmail.com


Printed in China by Shanghai Donnelley Printing Co., Ltd.

1   3   5   7   9   10   8   6   4   2

# LABYRINTH OF THE PAST

By Zhang Yiwei

Better Link Press

# Foreword

This collection of books for English readers consists of short stories and novellas published by writers based in Shanghai. Apart from a few who are immigrants to Shanghai, most of them were born in the city, from the latter part of the 1940s to the 1980s. Some of them had their works published in the late 1970s and the early 1980s; some gained recognition only in the 21<sup>st</sup> century. The older among them were the focus of the "To the Mountains and Villages" campaign in their youth, and as a result, lived and worked in the villages. The difficult paths of their lives had given them unique experiences and perspectives prior to their eventual return to Shanghai. They took up creative writing for different reasons but all share a creative urge and a love for writing. By profession, some of them are college professors, some literary editors, some directors of literary institutions, some freelance writers and some professional writers. From the individual styles of the authors and the art of their writings, readers can easily detect traces of the authors' own experiences in life, their interests, as well as their aesthetic values. Most of the works in this collection are still written in the realistic style that represents, in a painstakingly fashioned fictional world, the changes of the times in urban and rural life. Having grown up in a more open era, the younger writers have been spared the hardships experienced by their predecessors, and therefore seek greater freedom in their writing. Whatever category of writers they belong to, all of them have gained their rightful places in the Chinese literary circles over the last forty years. Shanghai writers tend to favor urban narratives more than other genres of writing. Most of the works in this collection can be characterized as urban literature with Shanghai characteristics, but there are also exceptions.

Called the "Paris of the East", Shanghai was already an international metropolis in the 1920s and 30s. Being the center of China's economy, culture and literature at the time, it housed a majority of writers of importance in the history of modern Chinese literature. The list includes Lu Xun, Guo Moruo, Mao Dun and Ba Jin, who had all written and published prolifically in Shanghai. Now, with Shanghai re-emerging as a globalized metropolis, the Shanghai writers who have appeared on the literary scene in the last forty years all face new challenges and literary quests of the times. I am confident that some of the older writers will produce new masterpieces. As for the fledging new generation of writers, we naturally expect them to go far in their long writing careers ahead of them. In due course, we will also introduce those writers who did not make it into this collection.

Wang Jiren
Series Editor

# Contents

# INTRODUCTION

I had always wanted to write about Xiaozha Town and Tianlin, up till now, when the town has completely disappeared, as if it used to exist only in a dream Shanghai locals would never wake up from. Torn down and reassembled, like so many side streets and alleys in Shanghai, it has been trampled over by time, as saddening as an unfulfilled whim from one's youth.

This feeling grips me whenever I hear Taiwanese reminisce about the Ximenting of their childhood, even though being an out-of-towner standing in front of the Red House Theater at Ximenting, I simply cannot conjure up the magic, electrifying and hormone-driven old times depicted by Luo Yijun and Wu Mingyi. All I know is that it has become a landmark for urbanites seeking the new, the bright, the lively and the bizarre. I asked some Taiwanese what it is that they like about Ximenting, or rather what it is that is special about that place. They told me that in the old times, every building in Ximenting was enshrouded in darkness and the twisted layout of the place appealed to the daring adolescents. Imagining themselves capable of every folly and excited at such thoughts, they snuck around that labyrinthine place, around heavily made-up older women waving from obscure archways and weird scheming older men littering the alleys. Smoky air reflecting off each face, they found in the place the answer to their reckless and adventurous adolescence. They found the place endless fun.

Endless fun, I wondered to myself. It is as if the lights on the opposite shore are but a blur to me. That is the same feeling I have today walking through the clean Xiaozha Town. I see no small-time vendors committing fraud in board daylight by rubbing golden powder on their oranges, no wild kids treading muddy roads in bare feet, no stalls selling fried pastry and pancakes. We keep all memories to ourselves, and the old times we have lived are now a fantasy we share with no one. I have a different labyrinth from my past, but I think of it with the same fondness. My history no longer has a mottled look. Instead it comes alive in my heart, asking to be preserved in that serene part of me.

I basically lived in the Tianlin area for an entire seventeen years, from age five to twenty-two. So all my memories and writings about Shanghai, as well as memories of my youth, originated there. For me, Tianlin New Apartment Complexes is an ever changing and developing hometown.

I am not making it up when I use the word "hometown". The Tianlin of my childhood was nothing but farmland. It is unconceivable now, but back then, every evening my mom would drag me through rows of pig pen to throw out the trash and empty the spittoon jars. I still remember smelling the pungent pig waste in the sunset. But I was always in a good mood and did not mind the smell at all. I actually demanded to go see the pigs every evening. Shanghai Sixth People's Hospital was yet to be built, although that river underneath the Yishan Road Bridge was already there, an opaque and stinky blackness. A lot of small boats docked on the river, and along the river was what was called Xiaozha Town. The Japanese author Teru Miyamoto wrote a river trilogy, and *Mud River* from the trilogy was adapted into a movie by Kohei Oguri. In the movie, kids from the town and kids from the river lay on the bridge counting the plying boats. Soaked by the occasional rain, the overjoyed kids jumped up and started running all over the place. Scenes like these are what I miss about Xiaozha Town. And the childhood captured in the movie has the same emotional undertone as that in my memory. The Yishan Road Bridge was not steep, but that did not stop me from feeling strangely elated whenever I went up and down the bridge sitting at the back of a grownup's bicycle. For a while I was very curious about how one could ride down the bridge with feet off the pedals, and delving into the vocabulary I had accumulated by then, I described the thrill from riding downhill as "fleeting" or "shot out like an arrow". Even when I was already in senior high school, my mom still had it in her to pedal me to math tutoring with a Shanghai High School teacher living on Wending Road. When I was a freshman at college, she switched to pushing the bicycle up the bridge. And we never walked the bridge together again after my junior year. She started taking the bus then, even if for just one stop. She would insist on accompanying me and we would get on the bus at the stop across from Sixth People's Hospital and get off at the lightrail station. Even without me sitting at the back of the bicycle, she could not have pedaled up the bridge. To all these desolate changes, the bridge bore witness. It has since been broadened and looks more like a boulevard wide enough to embrace all changes without panicking. Underneath the bridge still flows that Puhuitang-bound black river, a filthy presence that has survived all these years while everything else has changed.

Reportedly Xiaozha Town started having concrete roads in 1980, but in the eyes of Tianlin residents, it had always been dirty and disarrayed. There were the fruit wholesaler at the east end, Yishan Road bordering the west, and the House of Sheng at the south end. The streets were T-shaped and less than three meters wide. Puhuitang flowed through three towns, Longhua, Caohejing and Qibao, where a lot of immigrants congregated. What passed off as beautiful were a couple of ivy-covered small buildings in town center. The rest of the residential buildings would have been considered illegal nowadays, not a single one of which was decent, like today's slum on Hechuan Road. Xiaozha

Town maintained the same look even at the end of my childhood, the only change being that there were more people, streets became narrower, and the town became dirtier and less safe. In eighth grade, I went on a visit with the Students' Council from school to the Residents' Committee of Xiaozha Town, and the purpose of the visit was to help the poor. I have no fond memory of such a self-glorifying visit. All I remember was that the director kept emphasizing: "Here the crime rate has been dropping over the years." I was never victimized by any crime in the town, nor did I experience any of its rootless and crammed living or its poverty. I had but superficial knowledge of the hardships that made up the town. So how do I rationalize the overpowering nostalgia I have for it?

I actually did not live inside Xiaozha Town. I lived across from it on Yishan Road. We moved several times, but never far from this town inside the city. At the very beginning, we lived in temporary housing across from the end of Yishan Road, a transition offered by the Radio Plant. My mom said that the so-called roof for the temporary housing was a thin plastic board. The only way she could keep me cool in summer was to sit me in the red bathtub filled with water, not to bathe me but to preempt heatstroke. Even so, the roof turned burning hot, and I was told that the heat rashes on my forehead popped out one by one as if in an elaborate *Man and Nature* show in which one can witness how rashes grow, bloom and spread. And all my mom could do was to blow on my red forehead or to wave a fan. Life was as hard as that in the shacks of Xiaozha Town, but I still recall it with a fuzzy feeling.

The entrance to Xiaozha Town was on Yishan Road, and walking further towards West Zhongshan Road, one reaches what is today the Yishan Road lightrail station. In the early 1990s, there was a track frequently used by trains. Back then I never imagined not being able to see trains in Tianlin. Every time I crossed West Zhongshan Road, I would see a dozen or so bicycles stopped in front of the black and white bar. I do not recall that the grownups liked watching the trains, because being stopped for trains was undoubtedly disastrous for people with no time to spare. The same as when I walk down to the subway platform only to see the train pull away. My reaction is not "Let me admire the retreating back of the train", but "NOW I am going to be late for work". Back then I always sat at the back of a grownup's bicycle, listening to the bell ring, waiting for a train that would come roaring by, and getting as excited as if I was about to watch a show. Years later, in *How can a Snake Fly* written by Su Tong, I read about a man living next to trains and suffering from a weird physiological disease. Words from the book immediately conjured up for me the steel carriages galloping on Yishan Road.

As a matter of fact, Xiaozha Town was established in 1859, and its residents did not start relocating until 2005. So it was a presence throughout my adolescence. In our student days, we would make special trips to Xiaozha Town to play, because it was different from the organized apartment complexes for factory workers. There were many dilapidated buildings and country folks in the town, and we could see the chicken, ducks and geese they raised, and ferocious black dogs. The buildings were bare and on the verge of collapsing, since most of them were illegally built, the inside of which was impossibly twisted, rundown and filthy. Even in the late 1990s, there were still people cooking over a simple coal stove and making a living from it. The earliest pirate DVDs in Tianlin area were found there, too. Already in high school, I would still go there to buy DVDs with my classmates. Usually for 5 yuan, I could get ten to twenty episodes of Japanese or Korean TV on a condensed DVD wrapped in paper and sold in a plastic box. The DVDs were very blurry when played at home. I used to pick Takuya Kimura's shows and became a fan of this larger-than-life celebrity, even though on my 386 computer, he was but a mosaic image whose features I never got the chance to admire in high definition. That, of course, did not stop me from following the plotlines of his shows. It was always exciting going to Xiaozha Town to buy DVDs, especially after high residential buildings started springing up around it, leaving the town an isolated ecosystem inside the city. Kids felt like on an adventure going into the town to see some of the buildings that were stripped down with steel exposed. Some rooms in the buildings were piled to the ceiling, with kids bathing at the door and no sign at all of any imminent demolition. This kind of limbo lasted for quite a few years, until I refused to believe that Xiaozha Town would ever disappear from Tianlin. Then one day, the mess just went away, as if an eraser had been used to wipe everything clean.

Tianlin is an interesting place. Back then, Zhaojiabang Road cut it off from the city proper of Shanghai, and the area from the bustling Stadium to the desolate Caohejing belonged to Shanghai County. County comes with farmland and farmers, of course. After the Liberation, factories were moved from the city center to here, and apartment complexes for the factory workers were built, so the place took on a new look and a new mentality. The following thirty years saw impressive convenience-oriented development. In retrospect, Tianlin New Apartment Complexes could have passed off as a self-sufficient community. Hospital, school, park, hotel, department store—they were all there, so were farmers, factory workers, students, small-time vendors, and buses and trains, and even a crematorium close by. Kids had many places to play and grownups worked either at the postal factory or the Radio Plant, their jobs taken over by the younger generation once they got old. Young people from the city were sent to work in the county to experience so-called country life, and the intellectuals among them could choose to stay in the county or go farther to Pudong for farm work, temporary hardship that they knew would come to an end one day. In short, the lives of an entire generation unfolded within the community, from birth, to schooling, to working, to aging and to the eventual demise. And what's intriguing is that without having to venture much outside the community, that generation had been able to keep up with the times and seldom missed a beat. The down side was that the community was closed off and self-contained. My mom and my sister almost never stepped beyond Tianlin Road their entire lives, and my grandparents never left Tianlin after relocating there in the 1950s.

The other day I ran into Mr. Wu, editor at *Shen* newspaper. He reminded me that in the early 1990s, there was a direct bus route from Tianlin to Wujiaochang. I do not recall that. The Greater Yangpu area was almost an out-of-town place in my childhood memory. The bus routes I do recall were Line 89 to the Stadium and Line 93 to Xujiahui or Shanghai Normal University. After my mom signed me up for electric piano lessons at the high school affiliated with the Shanghai Conservatory of Music, we would take Line 93 to Fenyang Road and then walk to the school. But I do not remember which lines to switch to for the Bund or Yu Garden. We did not go to the city center often. Once a year we would visit the Sunrise Department Store next to the Stadium to buy new clothes and eat whipped cream. KFC came later and was a special treat for full scores on tests. In the early 1990s, the KFC store closest to Tianlin was the one next to Xuhui High School in Xujiahui which was also on the Line 93 route. I also remember going to play at Guilin Park and Nandan Park. My other recollections of Shanghai originated from TV and movies, like those of an out-of-towner. As for Tianlin New Apartment Complexes, it was not fashionable at all. It was not old-Shanghai either. It was a new being created after the Liberation.

After the 1980s, my grandma moved to Tianlin No. 5 Complex from Lane 65 on Tianlin Road. Four people crowded into one and a half rooms, with an extra room slapped together in the courtyard. My family also moved, from Yishan Road to Tianlin No. 14 Complex. So I was really close to my grandma's family when I was young, and my kindergarten was right next to Tianlin No. 5 Complex. My cousin and I used to lie on the tummies of my grandparents to watch TV, and I remember us scampering on the bed when watching that scary episode from *The Gods* starring Fu Yiwei, where a human heart was clawed out and human flesh was cooked into patties. Grandpa liked playing poker with us for fun, but he liked to cheat, too, hiding his bad cards under the table or between chair cracks. For a long time after he passed away, we kept finding cards he had hidden away. And that gave us mixed feelings.

On off days we would walk as far as Guilin Park for exercises and to smell the osmanthus there. Occasionally we would go to Longhua Temple to burn incense which passed off as a festive group activity. The tailor shops and rice shops around the apartment complexes are long gone now, and the Xinhua Bookstore on Tianlin Road was swept up by market development and replaced by a clothing store. The other day, the bookselling practice of open versus closed shelves inspired by Han Han's book took me back to my childhood which I miss dearly, as I have come to realize, especially as it ended soon afterwards. At the beginning of 1996, my grandpa passed away from a heart attack. He was only 59. People were just starting to relocate then, and our whole family went to check out the new housing at Pengpu New Apartment Complexes and almost decided on a place. Grandpa's death caught us off guard, followed by my father's leaving the family. My mom and I ended up making Tianlin our permanent home, and we became very stubborn about not entertaining any hope for changes or other impractical thoughts.

As a matter of fact, 1996 was a very important year for me, not so much because of my grandpa's death. Back then I was still apathetic towards death and understood little about pain and irreversible loss. What really struck me was that many strange things happened that year, including the departure of many kids from my school. They left Tianlin New Apartment Complexes with no intention of ever returning. Even several of my relatives left. So the security from a closed-off community and the sense of harmony and completion of my childhood evaporated. From then on, I started to see a clearer picture of the world.

The No. 3 Tianlin Elementary School I went to was located at the intersection of East Tianlin Road and Liuzhou Road, and one could reach it by going all the way through the No. 11 Complex wet market. I did not know until much later that the school was not a very good one. There was no social hierarchy back then, so parents did not have as acute awareness as today's parents of school districts, star schools, and quality of education and of the teaching staff. I remember our teachers being very interesting. There was this elderly Chinese teacher who was outraged by my test paper and sent me to time out. Usually well-behaved, I was seldom punished. So that day I couldn't stop crying, holding the test paper on which I wrote one Chinese character wrong: I wrote "river" for "lotus". I felt that I had committed the worst crime, with the teacher saying: "You don't even know how to write 'lotus'. How are you going to contribute to building the country in the future?" I blamed myself for a long time, and for the rest of my life, I will never forget how to write "lotus". I learnt later that the teacher, known to us as Ms. Yu, had "lotus" in her first name. So I guess she did not take kindly to people writing her name wrong.

There were many middle-aged teachers at our school who were more like aging neighborhood uncles interested in our daily lives, our parents' jobs and how many characters we could read and to which number we could count. They were not exactly what are called certified teachers today. My math teacher even taught my mom before me and remembered that she could sing well. As a matter of fact, during every lunch break, we would catch our teachers shopping at the No. 11 Complex wet market, and they even brought the vegetables back to their offices for cleaning behind closed doors. Then in third grade, we were assigned a new homeroom teacher, and rumor had it that she had an associate degree in teaching. I remember that she was very young and her name was Wu Jingxia. With a stern expression, she wrote on the blackboard "The silkworm keeps spewing silk till its death" from a poem by Li Shangyin. She said it was her motto and that we should copy it down. The kids in the class were at a total loss, and I kept looking up at the blackboard as all of the characters were very difficult and I had to draw them instead of writing them.

I did not know who Li Shangyin was, either. I just felt that this teacher was different from the teachers before her. She was very simple, serious and strange.

Our class was not on the fast track. I often fought with the boy sitting next to me. One day his water marker stained my clothes and I told him to get lost. He said indignantly: "Fine. I won't ever see you again after today anyway." I thought he was joking, but I really never saw him again. He moved to Italy with his family. Around the same time, the two kids sitting behind me moved too, one to Canada and one to Japan, and the girl across from me moved to Portugal. After the departure of so many classmates, the classroom felt empty to me, and I did not quite understand the social significance of their departure. Back then, there was no Internet or electronic devices, and we could read only a few characters. At the beginning, a few classmates who used to be close would send letters, short letters with Chinese pinyin mixed in them. They reported that at the foreign schools, they were required to learn *jiaoyi* dance and *jueshi* dance. It all sounded very strange to me, as I had no idea what *jueshi* dance was, either. At that time, we were still learning the song *Rain-Washed Stone* in our music class. Aqi, the girl standing next to me, asked me what the character was following "welcome". The character looked familiar, so I told her that it was "bustling" which was a really difficult character. She then asked what "bustling brightness" meant, and I replied that it probably meant the rain-washed stone led us to welcome a bustling and bright life. Once the teacher started to teach us the song word by word, we realized the characters actually read "welcome the dawning brightness".

Aqi was my good friend back then, and the reigning queen of our class. Everybody loved her, and even though I had higher test scores, I did not have any of the authority she had. The character Shen Jiayi from the hit Taiwanese movie *The Girls We Pursued Together in Those Years* many years later must have been modeled after Aqi. She was the one who hosted every class meeting, who raised the flag at school and who hosted the school radio station.

She had good scores, so did I. But I just wasn't on the same pedestal she was on, because her parents seemed to know the teachers very well. One time she came back from flying first-class with gifts for everyone in the class and perfume for the teachers, and we all voted for her from then on. Before graduating from elementary school, she was named an outstanding youngster of Shanghai and enjoyed a free trip to the American Dreamland in Shanghai. She really had all the glory.

The entire grade went through a reshuffle, and the kids replacing those who left were no longer from families of engineers and high school teachers. Instead they were kids of fishmongers in Xiaozha Town and vegetable vendors in the Tianlin No. 11 Complex wet market, a totally different breed. Dealing with them taught me one thing: once an era has passed, the rules of that era no longer apply. What bugged me were no longer trivial matters like my clothes being stained by water markers. The first thing I did coming back from PE class was to check whether my pencil case and school bag were still where I had left them, as they might have been thrown down the stairs by classmates who had fought with me. And I fought back by being equally violent. Those naughty kids knew how to push my button, of course. They often adopted a sarcastic tone towards me: "Do you think you are Aqi? So go tell on us like Aqi does."

For a while, the name Aqi evoked in me extremely mixed feelings. On one hand, I envied her and wished I could go with her to raise the flag, to play DJ at the Students' Council, to dance the group dance, to perform in the show from the Revolution era, to travel ... On the other hand, I did not want to ingratiate myself like she did. But I still tried to distinguish myself by imitating her, and it never ended well.

What my mom found strange was that starting fourth grade, I became a little rude and liked to talk back, and I had picked up some coarse slang. She was always correcting what I said like "nail it" or "quit it", words that she considered very bad for kids. And she almost fainted when I told her that I had been selected to play soccer at the junior sports camp and that the whole class had cheered for me. She rushed to school to shut the whole thing down, lamenting breathlessly: "Whatever you do, you cannot send my daughter to play soccer. What are you teachers thinking?" Because of her interference, I lost my authority in the class and was not re-elected to mid-level cadreship later. I was deeply disappointed, when I should have felt proud of my selection, since I had had to win a race to be selected and a lot of teachers had complimented me on my fitness and stamina. I remember that afterwards at Tianlin No. 7 Complex, I ran into the PE teacher who had taught me how to stand on my hands and to sprint. He was riding a big bicycle with his girlfriend sitting on the handle bar. It was the first time I saw a female grownup fitting onto the handle bar of a bicycle. Seeing me, the teacher rode off immediately. I felt that he must have really disliked me for my mom's stopping me from going to the junior sports camp. Around the same time, my mom was growing dissatisfied with my elementary school. Every time I told her about playing with Aqi, she would say poignantly: "Mom doesn't like you following others around. You are as good a kid as Aqi. Her family just has a small business, no big deal. We have decent background too, with all the workers in the family."

I did not quite understand then where my mom got the snobbishness that seemed to come so natural to her. At that time, she had not yet suffered the changing of times and the consequences of system transformation of state-owned workplaces. All I knew was that it would do me no good to compare with others and that my good scores were getting me nowhere. Walking back home from school every day, I would see Aqi's dad on the lookout for customers in front of the police station near Tianlin No. 14 Complex where I lived. Her family was selling deli at the entrance to the New Apartment Complexes, a business that was the most fashionable at that time. Reading *The Million-Yuan Household in Our Village* in *The Complete Collection of Student Essays* as a child, I would think of her family. She could play the piano and speak English, she travelled and celebrated birthdays at big rented places, she had tutu skirts and a gameboy—all of these sounded to me like "born with a silver spoon" as described in the books. But I refused to accept the hand I had been dealt. I felt that it was not difficult to measure up to her, yet I always fell short. I lived in Tianlin No. 14 Complex, too, and I could score high on tests, too. After elementary school, we went to different private schools and I had to study really hard to catch up. So it was not until then that I started to forget about her. Years later, after the Internet took over, I found her on Weibo (Microblogging in China) and learnt that she was working as a teacher managing CBA cheerleaders. Her most glorious moment was being a substitute cheerleader at a friendly game in Shanghai with NBA stars from the US. Nowadays she often complains online about how tiring it is to moonlight, her comfort being the audience's applause. It suddenly strikes a nerve inside me, but I just cannot put my finger on it.

I don't even talk to her, because something deeply saddening always stops me.

I don't think she still remembers my embarrassment about teaching her to read "bustling brightness". But she should still remember all the revolutionary songs we sang together as part of our patriotism education, because I do. Together, we also represented the school in the show *Legend of the Red Lantern*. We wore patterned cardigans and led the other students off the tempo of the show, for which we were scolded by the teacher. A lot of people doubted whether singing revolutionary songs was something my generation did, and I thought I might have just done it because it was fashionable. But looking at her pictures on the basketball court, I suddenly recalled the first time we walked through Xiaozha Town and took the bus to visit the Longhua Martyrs' Cemetery. I was so nervous and excited, and I asked her: "Are the red kerchiefs really dyed with blood from the martyrs?" She replied without hesitation: "Yes, of course." Suddenly I felt the same sadness that grownups would feel.

I still remember Aqi and I going home together after school, passing her dad's store on the way. She asked him to wrap up some delicious sausages for me before we crossed the street to play in Xiaozha Town, where we would watch the boats, watch the geese and watch the sun set. At that time, crossing the street was quite a challenge for elementary school kids like us. Although I was just a sidekick trailing the confident and almighty Aqi, I was happy and proud. The moms of our classmates living in Xiaozha Town would greet us even from a distance and offer food. I, of course, simply basked in the reflected glory from Aqi. Walking where we walked today, there is no glory to be reflected. Bare walls and a lonely river greet me instead. Human attachment which we once thought would last forever has disappeared with the disappearance of the dilapidated buildings.

More important, we all left Tianlin later. Silently. Social hierarchy becoming more pronounced and climbing the social ladder becoming even harder than moving abroad during an earlier time, people have less space and chance for building their dreams. Happiness is as rare as tears. What is left is the most mundane passing of time interspersed with regret and melancholy. Walking on the new but bare roads, I sometimes choke up at the sight of elementary school kids wearing red kerchiefs. But I know that they know nothing. And what they do know, no one after them will ever know.

August, 2012

# Scab Addiction

## 1

When it was inconvenient to do it at home, Puyue would boil the water outside and bring a stool to wash her hair at the street corner.

At age twelve, she was already too tall to wash her hair in a basin on the floor, otherwise she would resemble a lost chick soaked in boiling water when looking up abruptly. Still, she had fond memories of her childhood. She remembered squatting barefoot like a frog, swishing her long hair back and forth in the water in the basin. Out of the corner of her eye, she saw her parents hanging up a bedsheet. Their four limbs looked to her like tilted hairy table legs, and one didn't even have to see their faces to know that they were good folks.

It took her breath away recalling those moments, heart-warming moments that were gone forever. Or maybe it was just because however hard Puyue tried, she couldn't relive such moments, because the world was already upside down. Often, peeking backwards from her squatting position, she would see geese swaddling towards her. They seemed to have used orange cotton thread for eyeliner highlighting the deep blue of their eyeballs. Beaks a pouting cinnamon, they ran mindlessly, with a funny limp. Freaking out, Puyue shot up, kicked away the basin and ran for her life. This sudden movement made her so dizzy that she felt her soul escaped her for a brief second, in a world shaken loose as if by a careless hand with a glass ball. The water was spilled everywhere. And unfortunately for Puyue, she was still so young then and didn't run any faster than the geese. Her reactions weren't much smarter either, and the same maneuvers each time could have landed her in a jam, until either a grownup lifted her up, or she dashed inside whichever door was open and slammed the door shut, her soul barely following her. It was scary and thrilling at the same time.

Those geese loved harassing kids in Xiaozha Town, and kids fleeing the geese would bump into all sorts of things. It was routine to run for their lives several times a day.

Geese were by nature arrogant and aggressive. They were easily startled, as if they were the targets of persecution and bearers of centuries of class feud. Animals with bellies larger than their heads tended to not only hallucinate but to act out the hallucinations in strange ways. As a result, it was extremely dangerous for kids to play in Xiaozha Town without watching their backs. Abao, Puyue's one-time friend, had his penis bitten off by a goose while digging for earthworms with his butt in the air, after which his family moved way, broken-hearted. This incident put the entire town on high alert. Some couldn't wait to kill off the geese, and the following punishment was concocted for the one that took the actual bite: slicing its belly and stuffing it with dirt before sewing it up; sprinkling water on its feet before tying weights to them; hanging it from a beam and poking holes in its head to release its soul. The logic was this: the weights were gold, the beam was wood, the goose feet were water, its red beak was fire, and the stuffing in its belly was dirt. It was a diabolical scheme to condemn the geese forever and to deprive them of an afterlife. But it was also a very complicated scheme. So someone proposed simply killing the goose for food, better yet, killing and eating the entire flock. Eating the geese entailed dividing the meat which everyone needed to agree on. Having already moved way howling, Abao's family was out. The geese owner would rather not share the meat with other people. His own son had a good appetite, but he hated his guts and would have loved to starve him to death, so why would he feed him goose meat? Besides, there was no reason that the entire flock had to pay for what one single goose did. It wasn't the way of the new orderly society where one was responsible only for one's own actions. The geese owner ended up killing the offending goose. He poked its long neck with scissors without severing the neck, and with hands dripping goose blood, he brandished the goose around. Once everyone was satisfied at the sight of the mangled neck hanging together at the skin, the goose was dumped into a well. The well was thus destroyed and supposed to stink even worse than Puhuitang. But it was also said that the water already stank even before the deposit of the dead goose.

No one knew which town the goose moved on to haunt, Qibao or Longhua or Caohejing.

Just by listening to the wagging tongues, Puyue felt she suddenly started to know a lot of people in Xiaozha Town. Previously, people who looked familiar would greet her, but she couldn't tell them apart. After this incident, everyone seemed to walk around with a name tag and a certain expression for identification. The mastermind behind the diabolic scheme was the Jin family which rowed the boat for a living and lived on the boat too. People whose livelihood was tied to boats had this twisted belief that all sins were committed on land and water washed the sins away. The Li family owned the geese, and the son was a retard who was in heat all year long but missed being caught several times, which might have been a blessing for the family, or not. Afeng, cook at a small eatery, wanted the goose meat most. Since his wish was denied, he complained that the Li family's killing an animal in such a vicious way proved that the Li's were typical sociopaths from North Jiangsu. The one thinking the well was stinky was Yufen who lived next to the well. A young widow with a son, she was unbelievably aggressive. Every evening she would push out her cart to fry and sell radish puffs, and once she was in business, no one dared to set up the same shop within ten miles. But Yufen would quietly bypass Puyue's place every time, maybe seeing herself too good for the family. Anyway, grownups who had a role in the penis-biting incident had unmistakable identifiers afterwards, some of them talking in affected tones, some with exaggerated expressions. So it was that because of Abao's disabling, the human landscape slowly unfolded for Puyue.

As for the incident itself, it gave people something to gawk at and weigh in on. Some mentioned society, some blamed *feng shui*, and some had only one word for it: fate. Puyue asked Mom how Abao was going to urinate with the penis gone. Mom yelled her cross and cynical reply: "It's none of your business. You didn't bite it off, so no guilt trip there. Besides, it's just a penis, which might save him a lot of trouble later on anyway." Every time Mom lost her temper, Puyue didn't know what to do except to resent her. If she was honest with herself, on the day of the incident, both Mom and she heard Abao screaming, but she was washing her hair and Mom was inconvenienced as well, so neither of them rushed to his rescue. They could have helped Abao, and even though they were not really at fault, they couldn't mention it. Not being able to say anything didn't, however, erase it from Puyue's memory. She still blamed Mom to a certain degree. When he was still with them quite a while back, her dad liked to say that Mom was a master killjoy. He even had a term for it, "the founder of cold water pouring", coined from the term "the founder of aggressiveness" in the Shanghai dialect. Puyue didn't get what her dad was saying before she had learnt to write, but this term stayed with her throughout her childhood and was absorbed into the backdrop. Over the years, Puyue had come to realize how right her dad was. Mom was indeed a master killjoy. That was before she had to work. Now she only showed her true self off work, which suited Puyue well, since it meant fewer days a year she had to put up with Mom's stony face.

As for what Mom said about "it's just a penis", it sounded phony to Puyue even if it came from Mom. For a long time afterwards, Puyue thought Abao would have more than one penis, and with one gone, the others would grow out. That seemed to be Mom's message the way she talked about it. So no negligence when neither of them had rushed to Abao's rescue, and she should not have felt guilty at seeing what a wreck Abao was from between her wet hair hanging upside down and turning around to see a pair of hairy legs walking out of her own door. The only thought Puyue allowed herself was: "Fortunately I have no penis and there is nothing for you whitish grey ghosts to bite." At age twelve, Puyue still remembered Abao's looks. He was round every inch of his body: face, eyes, neck, arms, waist, calves and even the booger stuck above his upper lip. Penis was the only part of his body that looked pointed, and it ended up bitten off. Maybe fate had it that this protruding mallet should not stay to mar perfection. With its removal, he became a completely round object, one gushing blood at that. The young patriot who saved the day by urinating might have just looked like Abao, Puyue thought. But then, how could Abao not hate the whitish grey ghosts for the rest of his life? And how could it not be painful every time he urinated?

Puyue had no idea why white geese were called whitish grey ghosts. Old people might not want to say "kill goose" because it sounded like "kill me" in Chinese, but in Xiaozha Town, people no longer confused the pronunciation of "me" and "goose". Later on, several people did kill themselves, but it had nothing to do with geese, and they would probably have said "kill myself" instead of "kill me". Once people from South Jiangsu started calling "goose" goose and "me" something totally different, there was no danger of confusing these two at all. But people still tried not to say "kill goose". A lot of things made no sense.

The way Puyue saw it, Xiaozha Town was rid of white geese these years because after that incident, they didn't have it in them to run anymore and simply died of old age. However alert they were against people out to get them, they were but mortal. The leading goose whose stomach digested a penis and whose remains were dumped into a well, however, was different. The fate of the geese changed after its death, almost as if it was so aggressive as to drag the entire flock down with it. No hole was drilled into its head, instead its soul flowed from the hole-riddled neck, and with one breath, the water in Puhuitang was destroyed. And with another breath onto the rest of the geese, the flock met a peaceful end without even getting sick at first. With that, the incident was finally consigned to the deepest recesses of the memory. Things started to undergo subtle changes after that. The Li family opened a deli store on one end of Yishan Road, a full row of cooked geese dripping grease on the other side of the glass partition. A small fortune was made, followed by a new wife. The retard son, however, was bent on his luscious ways. Rumor had it that one day he was caught harassing female students at No. 2 Tianlin High School and threatened by bullies at the school, so he ran the distance of three bus stops from Liuzhou Road and jumped into Puhuitang next to Yishan Road. He died the laborious death of a typical retard. Already out of danger's way, he still hallucinated that someone was on his heels. He knew he was guilty after all.

The water in Puhuitang was already more than stinky. Loading up the boat, the Jin family was there to see the Li son jump into the water as if watching the TV series *Old Shanghai*. The only comment, heart-felt, was: "Man, it stinks ... Ah well, finally good riddance for the Li's." Hard to hear, it was nonetheless the truth. In Xiaozha Town, every family was an open book. Pains or grievances from a before life or this life were penned on big placards, with the end spelt out, too.

It hardly mattered that the death was indecent. Nor did it matter that Puyue's dad was in a lawsuit a while back. Xiaozha Town's regulars knew the ways of the world, and even though destitute, they understood when not to show mercy. The Jin family liked to say that the soul was a hair-like thread weaving through the heart and the lung. Hearing this, Puyue visualized a barbecue stick of chicken heart and lung in everyone's belly. And on that day, the soul of the Li son was hooked by a nail at the bottom of Puhuitang. One little tug and the thread broke, and his life was gone, his pains and grievances wiped out with it. Life was like the wind and the force diminished as life went on.

The stinky well was filled up sometime later. The stone road cracked open and was replaced by concrete before being paved over with cement. Puyue saw this as diabolic as the punishment concocted for the goose earlier. So the whitish grey ghosts must have put a curse on Xiaozhao Town, the way it deteriorated day by day. And the Jin family was behind it all, providing even the cement for paving over the road. The hole-riddled neck of the leading goose might no longer be capable of one more breath or one more spit, but the soul had beaten all odds and found an afterlife. When she was a little older, every time she went through the ritual of washing her hair outside, from carrying out the four-legged stool to adding coal to the stove, lighting and fanning the stove, putting on the copper kettle, waiting for the water to boil, pouring the water and burying her head in the basin placed on the stool, Puyue would think of those penis-eating whitish grey ghosts if she closed her eyes. Underneath Xiaozha Town, these ghosts were chatting non-stop and intimating the residents, and their beaks were not hammered but dyed red with Abao's blood. And their stomachs once ruined something very precious to someone.

But Puyue experienced neither fear nor nostalgia at such thoughts. Rather she found it strange that one could never forget some totally meaningless things in one's life and would even spice up such memories at will. It mystified her which rules people followed to screen out what to remember. The days would go on, going to school, going home, and eating and sleeping, with nothing out of the ordinary. But whenever she washed her hair, eyes closed and the sound of water in her ears, she would think of the geese and hear them running on clouds. She would think of their startled souls, and of them hobbling on the bridge of Xiaozha Town, clumsy and single-minded. She would think of them dying a speedy natural death. Condemned for having eaten a human organ, they died quietly and were dismissed as if they had never terrorized the town.

After moving away, Abao's family was soon forgotten. The Li son was soon forgotten, too, since he paid for his sins. Puyue's dad was guilty of similar sins, which were regarded in a gentler light after the Li family proudly welcomed a new wife. People started to gossip that had it happened a couple of years later, the sins committed by Puyue's dad would have passed off as indiscretions, and that he had been made an example of. But the same people gossiped earlier that he should count himself lucky to have dodged the death sentence.

A couple of years earlier, a couple of years later, sins or indiscretions, Puyue didn't care. All she remembered was that life started seeping out of Xiaozhao Town as if it had been torn apart by those incidents, big and small. The geese seen on the streets were bought from somewhere else, knotty necks dangling. Puyue sometimes thought that had Abao's penis grown back, Xiaozha Town would have been looking different.

She was just hypothesizing.

# 2

Xiaozha Town, where Puyue lived, was a strange place. At first glance, it was an alley in an ocean of mud. Back when Tianlin was still referred to as the Hongqiao Township, it was called Xiaozha Village. It lay south of the intersection of South Zhongshan Road and Yishan Road, Puhuitang cutting through the town, starting in the west and veering towards the southeast. If one bothered to look into its history, the town dated back to the reign of Emperor Xianfeng and was nicknamed Little Dam meant to stop the muddy tides. Boats would pass through the town just to load and unload. Leaders of the Brotherhood of Little Knives fought off the Qing soldiers here, a bloodbath like the ones recorded in the books. With so many more years of history, it was the ancestor to the workers' apartment complexes built in droves at the end of Tianlin Road. But dilapidation set in once the postal factory and the meter plant moved here and the workers' apartment complexes started filling up. The dilapidation took the form of chaos, migration and total purging of the original. Puyue was born amidst such unrest, under a solid brick roof. In summer, the whole family was trapped inside the airless room, counting the heat rash bursting open on each other's forehead. Puyue dreamt about moving to the workers' apartment complexes, like her classmates did, where reportedly one could wash hair in a separate bathroom, use a flushable toilet and cook on a gas stove. There were also ceiling fans and fragrant sprays.

She was just dreaming. In real life, Puyue wasn't so eager to get ahead. For example, she loved using tongs to push coal all the way down the stove, and she would moan upon hearing the coal at the very bottom crush. It was the same satisfaction she got from crushing waffles at the rice shop. Within a few short years, she had progressed from using both hands to hold the tongs to using one hand steadily, and from timidly rummaging through other people's trash for waste paper to asking her neighbor directly for wood shavings. She crushed countless amber coal, and lit countless fires in the stove.

On a good day, Afeng from the eatery next door would see Puyue out there trying to light the stove and would add some burning coal for her. That saved her a lot of time and trouble stuffing newspaper and wood shavings into the stove. But it wasn't something to be thankful for all the time, like when Puyue would get teary which wasn't necessarily a bad thing to her mind. The tears were caused by the smoke sometimes, and sometimes not. Delivering the coal, Afeng always asked her: "Washing your hair now? Someone visiting your mom again?" She would hide behind the smoke and pretend to cough. Afeng was the expert at lighting stoves including ice-cold ones. As a matter of fact, in Xiaozha Town, everyone seemed to need some non-essential expertise. Like Afeng, he could quickly tell where the wind blew and would simply put the coal right in the path of the wind and let the wind take care of everything. He was the cook in town but had more on his mind than cooking. During off hours, his eyes would dart everywhere, and a born busybody, he was first on the scene to help whichever family needed help. He kept his eyes open but the secrets he learnt open too, as if in the open diaries of a do-gooder.

Come to think of it, Puyue didn't find Afeng obnoxious at the beginning. She watched him grow up, from when he was already taller and faster than the geese and could easily lift her up and out of the geese's way, to after the geese had vanished and he no longer had to play her Ultraman, and to when he would bring out a cutting board everyday to chop up geese and chicken in full view of the live chicken and ducks. Bones and blood splattering onto his hair, nose tip and neck, like little moths, he didn't flinch and would even grin at Puyue. Puyue figured that Afeng's heart was stuffed with stiff rags, like the ones Mom left next to the wall, bloody and filthy rags that should have been kept out of sight. But he didn't know it himself and actually thought he was in the right. The worst thing about Afeng was his poking his nose into others' business. Puyue couldn't remember since when, but she felt naked in front of him. It wasn't a bad feeling in itself, except that he was different from others in her eyes. Puyue didn't like Afeng asking whether Mom was occupied, but there was no use trying to cover it. She accepted that in Xiaozha Town, he once stepped in as her Ultraman. He didn't exactly fawn on her, but he never mistreated her either. As for his obsession with other people's privacy, well, who wasn't obsessed.

Puyue could fill two and a half thermal bottles with every kettle of water she boiled. She would ask Afeng: "Do you want the other half bottle?" And Afeng would reply: "You exchange half a bottle of water for my hot coal. I am shortchanged. I want at least two and a half bottles." But that would mean that Puyue would have to give him all the water she used the hot coal to boil, which was pointless. Puyue of course didn't agree. Instead she picked up a black and cold coal to give back to him, without even bothering to say thanks. Afeng took it well, since she was still a child. So he just snickered: "Exchange a penny pincher for a whitish grey ghost, exchange junk for burning coal." Puyue liked hearing it, the first half sounding suspenseful and the second vivid. Sometimes she would tease him into saying it and felt let down should he forget to say.

After Puyue had washed and dried her hair, picked out all the hair on the towel, rinsed the towel, emptied the water, started another kettle, stared into space for a bit, added coal to keep the stove warm and filled the water bottles, Mom dragged herself outside to cook. It was hot and life was hard, so one was entitled to not feeling good. Puyue knew not to irritate Mom, since Mom never spoiled her anyway. She just accepted her presence out of instinct and seldom said anything important to her. When it came to important things, Puyue and Mom would tell nobody, because in the eyes of other people, they had a placard hanging in front proclaiming their boredom and hopelessness. Since her dad's lawsuit, Mom carried the family, and Puyue understood that Mom had no choice and had to feed herself.

Their dinner was simple, beans in soy sauce and fried eggs. Bent at the waist with her hand holding the bottom of the bowl, Mom accidentally showed half of one breast. Looking at Mom, Puyue felt helpless. Sometimes she found it incredible that one day that pair of lumps would grow on her chest, too. She witnessed how heat rash popped with an unstoppable force on Mom, but she wondered what extra force was needed for the chest to pop up so as to make the faint nail mark on it appear bewildering, jarring and raunchy against the setting sun.

"Jin is coming tonight," said Mom in a distant voice holding her bowl. A bean slipped from Puyue's hand.

"Oh. But the thermal inside of the water bottle is broken.

Can't keep the water warm. She likes hot water. I will get a new inside later," Puyue replied, which Mom didn't quite acknowledge.

Jin was sort of a sister to Mom, and not much younger, although she insisted that Puyue call her older sister.

"She isn't staying with Tuchui?" asked Puyue.

Mom replied: "Who knows. Wait till she gets here."

"Tuchui" was Minnan dialect that Puyue picked up from Jin. She had no idea what it meant, so it could be a bad word. Jin used it to describe the Taiwanese old man she was going out with, and Puyue used it to describe Abao. She figured that whatever they were, words were meant to be spoken. Memory was just endless words sounding strange before becoming familiar and interspersed with nonsequential acts. Puyue had never met Tuchui, but she had recollection of the Tuchui in her mind's eye. She once saw the taxi stopped at the end of the alley in Xiaozha Town, a new and fashionable accessory for a mysterious, rich and dumb out-of-towner. He wasn't just the stereotypical Taiwanese hillbilly, but a real presence linking Jin and the fate of Puyue's family.

Mom did get to meet Tuchui. She took a taxi with Jin to Qianhe Hotel. Before they floated into the car, Jin was loudly saying that one could tell Shanghainese by whether they could pronounce the word *he*. Taiwanese couldn't, although they could handle stranger pronunciations such as *nuan nuan*. Muttering this pronunciation, Puyue took the stove out to light up. *He nuan he nuan he nua*n, she was actually mixing up two unrelated pronunciations. Afeng had gone shopping, so no hot coal to get Puyue started. She looked around for where the wind blew, trying to mimic Afeng's gestures and feelings, but ended up choking on the smoke and choking back the *he* pronunciation, her mouth all scrunched up to the point of puking. Yufen was across the street with no customers. Flour spread out before her and soup simmering, she fixed Puyue with a cold stare. Puyue suddenly felt a little silly.

Mom said that Tuchui looked well-kept, like a capitalist, with a protruding belly. Puyue couldn't imagine her dad with such a belly, since he was taken away before reaching the fattening middle age. Puyue was just pleased that Mom's comparing Tuchui with her dad meant she hadn't forgotten the family ties.

Mom also brought back pastry with pineapple filling given by Tuchui, for Puyue's breakfast, declaring that it wasn't nearly as good as pastry with shell-shaped crust or cut out like butterflies. She talked about Tuchui as if they were already close friends, without any rancor. Puyue asked: "What shell-shaped crust?" Mom replied: "It makes the pastry yummy." Puyue then asked: "As yummy as the fried puffs?" Mom replied: "A lot yummier." And Puyue asked again: "Isn't capitalist supposed to be a bad person?"

Not having the same nimble tongue, Mom couldn't keep up the argument and grew a little sullen. Since her dad's departure, Mom hadn't been all smiles towards Puyue. She had to stick with the family, like a widow, but without as much to fall back on as Yufen did. Jin often said she should have aimed higher, but Puyue disagreed and disliked such condescension towards Mom. Besides, she loved Mom and learned things from her that she could hardly forget. For example, Mom would pull from around her waist crimson and stiff cotton balls and tell Puyue that a woman would bleed copiously in her pants when unhappy, and the hardened blood would stick to the softest skin causing the skin to bleed at the slightest touch, and one couldn't tell if the blood was real blood or unhappiness that had bled out. But it was no big deal. Puyue was scared witless, but back then, her unhappiness wouldn't have been that extreme.

For a long while, it was as if Tuchui had been living with Puyue's family. Puyue used some of the small things he gave them, and some were handy enough to be brought to school. Tuchui was a relative one never got to see, and neither Puyue nor Mom disliked him. He maintained an unreal presence in their lives, bringing them gifts from time to time, like Santa, especially with the reportedly protruding belly. In her sincere moments,

Mom would wish that Jin had done better for herself, thoughts that weighed her down, especially as according to Jin, Tuchui felt guilty and saddened that she never mentioned marriage or demanded that he divorce his wife. He planned to buy Jin a big place worth half a million.

Half a million. Mom speculated to Puyue: "Hope Jin didn't sell any state secrets. She isn't the smartest pea on the pod, and she must have said something without thinking and been taken advantage of. She never thinks about what happened to her dad. My goodness, it's too scary."

Half a million, Puyue did the math. Yufen's fried puffs sold for ten cents each, and Afeng's goose neck for one yuan and fifty cents a plate, would all the brick buildings in the whole Xiaozha Town add up to half a million?

So, Puyue suddenly concluded, Jin must be a bad seed.

Puyue's family moved to Xiaozha Town on a summerlike day in autumn, which made one feel out of sorts. Some years later, two apartment buildings sprang up in Xiaozha Town, towering over miles of low and rundown housing. Every eye in town, human or animal, stared at these two strange buildings, just because they were different and an eyesore. Then the roads got dug up and filled in again. The construction of the new housing seemed to be following a meticulous scheme which no one had bothered to announce, and life in town didn't appear any different from before. So what kind of people would be moving into these two new buildings? No factories were being built in the neighborhood, which added to the mystery, for the old people, and even more so for people like Puyue.

Jin originally lived in the brick building closest to the two new buildings. Mom would refer to her as living where the new housing was. When Shanghainese spoke of new housing, there was an intonation of newlyweds. So at the beginning, the name Jin sounded auspicious to Puyue.

Mom said that the first time she saw Jin, she was being

kicked out by her husband and at her lowest. In the middle of frying her puffs, Yufen from next door looked at Jin askance and told her not to block the way for business. Jin went up to Yufen and kicked her stove, demanding: "What's a bigger deal, wife beating or playing widow? You sleep with your stove at night now, but weren't you sleeping with a retard before?" Enraged, Yufen threw a ladle of half burning oil onto Jin's leg. Jin's husband took off to Japan with half of the money that Yufen later loaned from her parents to pay Jin's medical expenses. Had it not been for the money, he would not have left the country, and Jin's life might have been different.

So Jin's life was ruined by Yufen, and Yufen's by the Li son who died a long time ago when there were still geese in Xiaozha Town and he jumped into Puhuitang and turned the water stinky. All of these felt like a century ago even though they were actually quite recent. Mom said that it was Puyue's dad who called a pedicab that day to take Jin to the medical center before infection set in. Puyue's family saved Jin's leg.

Abao was unlucky, Puyue thought. He missed the good times when her family played savior.

Jin moved, reportedly to a condo on Weining Road. Tuchui lived there, too. Puyue didn't know what a condo was. She figured that one level up from the brick buildings were the new apartment complexes where a lot of her classmates lived, but kids from there wouldn't play with them. Only a handful of kids lived in Xiaozha Town, but she didn't walk home from school with them. It might look like that she knew quite a few people, but besides Mom, only Afeng and Jin bothered to talk to her.

Puyue wondered whether the bad woman in the TV series *Silver Fox* lived in a condo. She recalled that there was a bottle of fragrance on the dresser of the Hong Kong star. Steam would encircle her in shower, turning her into a fairy from Chinese folklore. Why did Jin come back if she was already living in such a nice place, Puyue wondered. But then her thoughts immediately took off in another direction, which was strange.

Every day after dinner, Mom would hold her hand and take her across the street to empty out the spittoon. Farmland stretched out to the south of the intersection of West Zhongshan Road and Yishan Road, and pig pens took over farther on. Puyue loved watching the pigs. For a good number of years, Mom would let her have her way. While Puyue played, Mom would wait sitting on the portable toilet with the lid on. Mom always looked tired while waiting and complained of back pain after standing on her feet for longer than she had to. Sometimes at home she would hold onto the bed and exercise her back strenuously. Puyue never asked her why and never found out whether she had back problems. She just prayed for Mom's health the same way she prayed for her dad's early return. It could have all been wishful thinking.

While Puyue was playing with the pigs, Mom had enough time to tuck in her hair and clothes, absent-minded and slow about it as if she was merely looking for things to occupy herself. She looked contented waiting for Puyue, as if she had always been contented with a lazy life. Not a word was spoken as she basked in the setting sun. Farmers wouldn't come out to collect manure until very late. Mom would just sit patiently, looking lonely and a little expectant. The portable toilet of Puyue's family was small but frequently used. When she was a bit older and had to carry the heavy toilet alone across the field, Puyue realized how pathetic Mom was.

Since a young age, Puyue had looked forward everyday to accompanying Mom to empty out the portable toilet, because that was the only time for unadulterated happiness for her. She saw Mom at her prettiest sitting all neat on the toilet in the sunset, prettier than even Jin with her fragrance. Even though she didn't speak, light sparkled in her eyes and on her brows. It was so different from when she was squatting on a low stool and eating beans from the bowl in her hand, and no deformed breast peeked out. Once they got back to Xiaozha Town, Mom's beauty was nearly erased, and whatever was left took on a bloody smell, like the smell of human blood around the goose's beak and of cotton balls against the wall.

Puyue's mental image of Mom was the opposite of that of Jin.

Jin didn't look like she ever needed cotton balls her entire life, what with her exuberance. But however smooth sailing life was, once in a while she would come back in five-inch heels, pull down her skirt and beat everyone to the clean toilet at Puyue's place. She was of the real calculating kind. Puyue didn't like Jin, but Mom asked her to be nice to her since she gave them a lot of good things, like Mom's stockings and lipsticks, little paper umbrellas that Puyue could stick into shaved ice, long plastic spoons, imported marshmallows and fancy colas. Puyue of course understood that these things were hard to come by. It was never easy for anyone to step outside Xiaozha Town and come back with some decent things. Still, Puyue loathed Jin for being selfish.

Jin always knocked on the door after three in the morning. Mom would open the door for her and they would check each other out, like they always did, enveloped by endless rustling sounds.

Puyue turned her face towards the innermost wall, faking deep sleep. But she was assaulted by the fragrance. She figured Jin must be using hot water from the new thermal inside to wash, but the fragrance simply couldn't be washed off. Things that one lingered onto would linger on. Puyue heard Jin talking animatedly to Mom and imagined her taking off her skirt at the same time, lifting up the toilet lid and plopping down on the seat once satisfied that it was empty. Bowel movement. Acting as if it was perfectly normal. Urination. Hearing the sound, Puyue felt like Jin was urinating on her head. She believed that Jin had it all planned out, because even though she wouldn't leave until after noon the next day, after having put on makeup, she would never use that waste-filled toilet again, for a dozen long hours.

She was originally from Xiaozha Town anyway, so why act as if she was better. That's truly detestable.

Tormented inside, Puyue kept her mouth shut and her ears open for breathing and sighing around her. She couldn't help still feeling curious about Jin.

But apparently, that night Mom and Jin didn't openly discuss anything important. The light was turned off after Jin had washed her face and feet. The three of them lay in bed and no one was able to fall asleep.

Jin and Mom whispered for a bit. Puyue heard Mom say: "That's really nuts." and was suddenly intrigued. Puyue knew that Mom liked talking to Jin. Like the time when she took Tuchui's money, while he was out of town, for plastic surgery for double-fold eyelids, Jin came to Puyue's place for recovery. For several days her eyes were almost swollen shut and she couldn't take care of herself. At least she was grateful and didn't forget to leave Mom some monetary compensation, while whining about the pain. Mom called her nuts then, in a very intimate tone.

It was from Jin that Puyue learnt one could go under the knife for double-fold eyelids. After the surgery, Jin looked stiff and funny, but Puyue had to admit that she did become much prettier. With her beauty wish granted, she turned arrogant. After the swelling had gone down, she studied Puyue with disdain and commented: "Your eyes are deep set too and look triangular if you squeeze the lids." With the swelling gone, the surgery marks were now visible. She couldn't see them herself, so she acted as if she had been reinstated as the maitre d'hotel of Lan Dai. This whole thing really put Puyue out.

Since Jin started the new job, Puyue picked up some details of her life which presented a new world more vibrant and picturesque than Xiaozha Town. Quite a few times she dreamt about waking up in a private room at Lan Dai, alcoholic vapor rising from the carpet from women that Jin would call princesses and that looked in the dream like fairies from Chinese folklore. As if through a veil, she saw those women kneeling to pour the wine till four in the morning, by which time their legs already gave out and they had to sit on the floor with uncertain smiles.

Puyue dreamed about saying: "Come, give me the bill." before everything blurred out and numbers started flying everywhere.

Those women had no time to remove makeup. They drank till they were numb, then they sat around, distant and hallucinating, like mannequins. These were the kind of scenes that rolled off Jin's tongue, but Puyue felt that she actually lived them. But then Jin would pull her out of the trance by starting to lecture her on wearing bras. Mom would overhear that and blame Jin for acting nuts. Jin would retort: "Don't be naïve. You really expect her to become an intellectual? Intellectuals are useless nowadays and can't even compare with Li selling whitish grey ghosts across the street."

"Nuts," Mom repeated without getting mad. She just told Puyue not to listen, because she needed to keep her mind clean.

Apparently Mom understood Jin's predicament better than Puyue and dreamt no dreams after listening to those strange tales. She never told Jin to change her way of life, which seemed to be a warm tacit agreement between them. Jin wouldn't have been able to remarry anyway even if she were to break up with Tuchui. The more one thought about it, the more doomed Jin appeared. To Mom, Jin was weathered, whilst she and Puyue were trapped. No one could tell which was a better lot. Hope was often bred in despair, and a stable life void of all excitement could wear one down.

Puyue asked what Jin's own family was like. Mom said that Jin's dad was branded a rightist during the rectification period, even though he wasn't a real rightist. His gravest sin, however, had nothing to do with left or right. It was that he would never admit to having fathered Jin. "It's good that he was never acquitted," said Jin. "There were so many rightists. Acquittal was necessary, but too bad he missed the boat. Someone has to have all the bad luck, the way of the world, so no big deal that a heartless fake rightist didn't get his acquittal. I'm family and I get it." Mom couldn't stop laughing at the words "I'm family" and started calling Jin nuts again, adding that she loved where no love was to be found. Animals with bellies larger than their heads were like that, goose and human no exception. Jin would recount these things as if telling jokes, emotionless. And when it came to her mom, Jin was more reticent. "She was silly," was all she would say.

Mom said that Jin's mom would have found comfort in seeing how Jin had turned out. Jin was a survivor who had saved herself for her husband despite a childhood spent almost as an outcast. The first half of her life wasn't much different from Puyue's, and her future looked much brighter than Puyue's as far as Mom was concerned. Life was getting harder as society was opening up. No light at the end of the tunnel.

Jin ended up pawning in the black market the jewelry her silly mom had left her for her wedding. Then someone got her a job at a nightclub called Lan Dai where she got to see more of the world courtesy of businessmen from Taiwan and Hong Kong and Shanghainese who had came back from Japan. Jin said that *tuchui* meant a braggart in Shanghai dialect. Taiwan or Shanghai dialect, neither word made much sense to Puyue.

"Also," Puyue asked Mom, "what is a rightist?"

Mom said that it was outdated and that it once referred to a bad person.

# 3

Mom being friends with Jin, Puyue often snuck around them trying to catch what they were saying, after which weird dreams would visit her, out of her control. In those dreams, either she was poking at the floor with her fingertips till wine starting flowing up at her, or Mom was holding onto the bed for her rehabilitation exercises of squatting and standing up. She was bewildered and pleasantly surprised by all of these, while a little upset which she couldn't tell why.

It wasn't just Puyue. Everyone kept track of Jin's comings

and goings. She was originally from Xiaozha Town, so people cared to know when she was coming back. She married a boatman at eighteen, so the Jin family knew her and the two families were once close. The Jin family might have said that all sins were committed on land even though the actual death was in water. Jin's husband went to Japan later, which was the trend then. He became an illegal immigrant who either died there or was recruited by gangs. So divorce was just something Jin said herself. She was never divorced and could never remarry. She was totally comfortable with this fact, although no one else was. Time passed and a lot of important things became not so important anymore. For Jin, the wife-beating husband was eroded by time to oblivion, like a fish bone stuck in a non-fatal position in the throat.

Jin did differ from Mom, in that she had been intimate with only one man in Xiaozha Town. And that man had disappeared. His soul was hooked somewhere else instead of at the bottom of Puhuitang. Things were looking up for Jin as society was becoming more tolerant and she did have new looks. But when she was down and no one would offer any help, Mom let her stay with them, seeing her own misfortune in her. She was almost hysterical trying to return the favor, buying Mom coffee at the Qianhe Hotel opened by a Taiwanese businessman on Tianlin Road, taking her on taxi rides, and admonishing her to divorce the sexual offender of a husband. Loyalty and forgiveness weren't in Jin's dictionary, and she tried to impart the same philosophy to Mom and didn't mind if it happened to rub off on Puyue.

Jin would tell Mom: "I have no choice, but you do. You can get a divorce and come with me to Lan Dai. You still have a few years in you." Mom wouldn't agree. She knew it wouldn't end well with Puyue's dad, but she still wanted to wait, which she kept to herself because it wasn't something to boast about. Mom felt she had committed graver sins than Puyue's dad, but he was the one serving time. All she could tell Jin was: "I can't do what you do. I am not like you, I am short." Hearing this, Puyue had this sudden desire to grow tall, as a taller Puyue might have a better shot at living in a condo which would have more than made up for a scarred leg.

The world had changed, and the entire Xiaozha Town was quite smitten with Jin. The consensus was that Jin was fashionable and must be living in a place even better than those two workers' apartment complexes next to the bridge. But exactly how better, no one could tell. People just regarded Jin more kindly than they did Puyue's family. Once she starting bonding with Puyue's family, it was taken for granted, since there was clearly empathy between them. Besides, birds of the same feather, people rationalized.

So it was that Puyue was at the receiving end of the evil eye, too. And alienated. But back then she didn't feel wronged. Her heart was a clean landscape of endless farmland, a night light resembling the setting sun and a silhouette staring into desolation. She would light the stove and cry smoke-induced tears, and boil some water and imagine the world upside down in the steam. Everything felt unreal. Behind closed eyes, Puyue could see her childhood, the four feet on the bedsheet, vivacious geese and a chubby Abao lost in digging in the dirt before being attacked.

Only at times like this did Puyue feel that whoever could treat her like a normal child had to be extremely kind.

With Jin staying so often at Puyue's place, the two families' belongings got mixed up. Jin had a pair of worn red shoes bought when she first met Tuchui. Tuchui was shorter than Jin, so Jin never wore heels for their rendezvous. She had long abandoned the shoes at Puyue's place. Puyue laid eyes on them, patent leather, flat heels, with butterflies adorning the toes. Not knowing that they were badly worn, Puyue loved the shoes, and smuggled them out the door one day when she saw that Mom was about to get busy. She was elated at putting them on. Afeng was leaning against the eatery door and asked her when he saw her come out: "Your mom got something going on?" Puyue couldn't have been more nervous wearing the red shoes. Afeng went on to mention that he was heading to the fruit wholesaler east of town to pick up things for fruit salad and asked whether Puyue would like to tag along. Of course Puyue would, with the red shoes. And since she had nothing to do anyway.

On the way there, she was able to keep up with him and his questions. After Afeng had got his supplies and was about to head back, it started pouring. The roads in Xiaozha Town were paved over, but still turned muddy in the rain. Puyue walked slower and slower following him, and when passing those two new buildings, she suddenly felt bittersweet. The shoes were one size too big and extremely slippery if she didn't watch her steps, so she tripped quite a few times. Puyue grew nervous and wondered whether she should simply take off the shoes, but it was too dirty to walk barefoot. She was desperate to walk faster to catch up with her companion, but her feet refused to cooperate. Not only that. The pretty shoes were soiled which Mom would surely notice when she got home. She didn't know what to do.

At that moment, Afeng turned around and saw how far behind she had fallen. He had his usual smile on, raindrops hanging all over him. They were both at a loss for words. After staring at her from the distance and realizing that she really had no strength to walk anymore, Afeng turned back.

Puyue was in fifth grade then and reached only Afeng's chest when face to face with him. They stood like that for a while, Afeng holding a plastic bag that was soaking wet and weighing down on his fingers till they were a soaked red.

Puyue thought about it, a warm sensation swelling up in her. Finally she took one of Afeng's hands, and Afeng naturally held her hand back.

Puyue's shoes seemed to fit all of a sudden, and all kinds of questions and answers took over her being. She realized that holding hands with someone for the first time was very important, but she told herself that it didn't count this time, since she had no choice. She also realized that she had misbehaved by wearing the wrong-size shoes, but she also told herself that it was no big deal.

This was the first time Puyue wasn't looking from between her pants at a world that was upside down while wearing wet hair. It felt really good. With her head held high, she dragged the red shoes through rain water, strangely calm and all innocence. The two of them held hands and walked past the new housing, over the bridge and over Puhuitang where someone had once drowned, and past many households. Not a single unhappy thought intruded.

They also walked past Yufen in the middle of packing up her cart. With a dejected look, she was putting away the stove, since soaked white flour wouldn't taste good. Puyue suddenly felt like gloating, shooting a glance at Yufen. Yufen was stealing a look at her at the same moment.

Afeng asked: "Puyue, why did you wear your mom's shoes?" Puyue laughed, but had no reply.

It was an unforgettable day, dreamlike. Lying half asleep next to Mom and Jin, Puyue dreamt that Afeng asked again: "Puyue, why did you wear your mom's shoes?"

# 4

Mom and Puyue got up early next morning. Puyue cooked the leftover rice before getting ready for school. Despite her back pain, Mom washed everyone's clothes including Jin's stockings, panties and bra. It was nothing unusual, since Puyue had come to see Jin as a special presence in her family. Jin filled in for her dad, so there were still three in the family. They sought the best in each other for their co-dependence.

Jin was easygoing and nothing could deprive her of sleep. And she hogged the bed. It was hot and her leg stuck out from under the comforter, burn scars stretching all over as if on a map. Without those scars, her eventful past would have been totally obliterated from her memory. But out in the world, those reminders of pain could get in the way. So Jin wore grey and black stockings and long skirts all year long, at work or off and however hot it was. It was only at Puyue's place that she could let the guard down.

Jin left a lot of her pretty long skirts at Puyue's place. She had no intention of getting them back, since tailors in Xiaozha Town could no longer satisfy her. Mom wasn't sure if Jin still wanted those skirts and would put one on when she was in a good mood. But she had a smaller behind and waist and was shorter, so dressing up Jin's way turned her into someone all dolled up to burn incense at a temple. She could, however, use Jin's abandoned bras, matched with her own pants, or rather mismatched. Mom was picky about certain things and not picky about others, a line that was apparently well defined for her.

Jin seemed to be seductive, the way she slept. The Li son climbed into her bed once, was kicked off and got away. No longer a virgin by that time, she went back to sleep, not at all disturbed. When the Li son died, Jin said that he went the same way as that person in the broadcast, "Li, Li something, right, Li Xiannian". The Li's seemed to be having a tough year, which wasn't entirely true, since Deng Yingchao passed away the same year. Puyue had no interest in anything in the broadcast, and from the whole Li family incident, she only remembered the name of the school, No. 2 Tianlin High School. She figured it must be a bad school where people were even more vicious than Jin and would gang up to literally kill someone.

Once she was assigned by the computer to that high school, she was calm. She recalled the day she was notified. She went back home to wash her hair, courtesy of hot coal from Afeng. Afeng asked the usual question: "Someone visiting your mom?" It had never sounded harsher to her ears.

Puyue kept quiet.

Afeng said again: "Oh, why are you crying? Is it the smoke?"

Puyue still wouldn't answer.

She finished boiling the water. Standing and bent forward

for the wash, she suddenly saw the boil on her chest underneath her tenting T-shirt. Panicking, she tried to cover her chest and ended up getting soapy water all over herself. Afeng must have taken in everything. He smiled and left.

It was an unforgettable scene. Soap on her head and hands on her chest, Puyue looked like a lost chick.

Afeng came out again with a stool and cutting board to chop geese. Business as usual without another glance at Puyue.

So don't look at me, Puyue thought to herself. She wouldn't want Afeng to look at her all the time, even though in her mind's eye, she had always been naked in front of her. Timid and helpless.

There were many last-minute compromises in one's life, and pressing situations that one had never anticipated. After all, Puyue didn't quite get how different No. 2 Tianlin High School was from No. 3 Tianlin High School or from any other high school for that matter. Once she started going there, no one seemed out to get her. She actually quite enjoyed walking from Xiaozha Town to Tianlin Road. There were many routes, and which one to take was food for thought on the way to school and back. Like when Mom told her she had to work, she would take a detour. She would go to the Metallurgy Professional School or Guilin Park where she would sit for a while and wait for the sun to set, like when Mom was sitting on the portable toilet, her heart so peaceful and open that she could hear a needle drop.

Puyue had no company for her detour, and no one seemed to want to keep her company. Sometimes she knew why, and sometimes she didn't. Leaning on the bridge railing over Puhuitang, she saw that the Jin family's boat couldn't even be started anymore, the Li family's store was prospering, and Yufen had lost all interest in her. Melancholy overwhelmed her. She couldn't tell good people from bad ones, but she knew that outdatedness was everywhere. For example, the sanitary napkins Mom got from Jin and hid away like a treasure. Puyue stole one from her and it looked like a butterfly.

She felt that she was becoming outdated herself. Her feet

were growing bigger, but she was growing less inclined to even look at that pair of red shoes.

## 5

She slept through the night, but watchful subconsciously, and somewhat suspicious and anxious. Dreaming about what Afeng said added a sense of loss. She couldn't concentrate on her books the whole day. Wandering about, she even counted on her fingers to the day her dad would come back. It seemed to be a taboo at her place, not to be spoken of, and not even to dwell on too much mentally.

Puyue didn't get home till the sun had set. Seeing the low fire in the stove, she naturally shot a glance at Afeng's empty eatery next door. For reasons she couldn't explain, she felt a mysterious connection. Suddenly nervous as if a goose had bitten on her chest, she had the urge to poke her head in Afeng's store.

At that moment, a familiar figure popped into sight, the Ultraman turned monster. Passing in front of Puyue, he looked exhausted and gratified. Seeing her, he was suddenly embarrassed before squeezing out a dry smile which was totally different from the warm smile stored away in Puyue's heart.

More important, he didn't even ask her any question.

When Puyue pushed open her own door, Mom was pouring water to wash herself, the copper kettle beside her. Seeing her daughter, she quietly moved to a shadowy spot and said: "Done with school?" Puyue saw some bloodless cotton balls next to the wash basin.

Already dejected, she felt tears at the back of her eyes. And she was a little tired. She never liked the Mom in Xiaozha Town and felt that the woman washing in front of her was a different person from the Mom who crossed to that side of Yishan Road in her childhood. This feeling was especially pronounced today, and she found Mom irritating.

Puyue tried to move the portable toilet which was really heavy. Mom took that moment to say: "Tuchui is so nice. He really bought Jin a place before returning to his Taiwanese wife. Jin said that we can visit her at her place in the future. I still worry for her and can't help thinking that she betrayed our country. Ha, how silly I am. A lot of things are beyond me now. Are you happy? We can go see her at her new place." Mom looked in a great mood and words came gushing.

"New place."

Puyue should have felt happy for Jin. Jin had been decent to her. She kicked over Yufen's stove, and Yufen had always looked down on Puyue's family. In Xiaozha Town, it wasn't every day that one person got to witness another person reaching the end of the tunnel. How come Mom couldn't have waited for the end of her tunnel. How awful.

Puyue suddenly asked: "Mom?"

Mom stood up, tying her pants.

Puyue asked: "Was it … Afeng next door who just came by?"

Mom asked: "Why?"

Puyue replied: "I want to get some coal from him."

Mom asked: "For what?"

Puyue replied: "Washing hair."

"How about tomorrow? Why do you like washing your hair now? We used to wash once every two weeks," Mom replied.

Puyue asked: "So he really came to our place? What did he want? It's late and he has the eatery …"

Mom replied: "… Why are you crying?"

# A Good Year

## 1

The first time I brought Zhuoran home was February of last year. I didn't tell Mom beforehand, nor would I have known how. I simply mentioned to her one morning: "I want to bring a friend home one of these days. Can you take a break and come home around noon?" Mom was on the floor wiping away. She said without pausing to think: "No. It's almost New Year and getting busy at the shop."

At that time, she was working at a privately owned photo shop, cutting the photo paper, setting up lighting, keeping an eye on the shop and cleaning the shop. Since her early retirement, she had been spending a lot of time at this photo shop, but I still couldn't see any deep connection between her and photography. She did like having her pictures taken and had kept a lot of pictures from different times and by different photographers. Some of them were art lovers from the factory's labor union, some were young guys from the next workshop, some were distant relatives, and some were leading entertainers during her years laboring in the countryside. She said that those pictures had been taken for me so that I wouldn't miss her too much once she was gone. But she seemed to have started this prep work as a young girl. Coloring wasn't available in those years, and the pictures were no bigger than a fingernail. But she still glued them into the albums, noting the time, place, photographer, and the style and color of her clothes beside each tiny picture. I asked her the whereabouts of those photographers, and she looked lost at not being able to tell. The floodgates re-opened once we moved on to anecdotes during the photo sessions and how to strike poses. Even though she never figured out how to turn on a digital camera or learnt the first thing about Photoshop, I believed that those pictures and experiences had become an indelible part of her life.

Her reply being so firm, I didn't have the heart to disrupt her rhythm. So I had to tell Zhuoran: "Why don't you come in the evening? My mom is busy and maybe we will have to make do with a simple dinner." Zhuoran agreed readily and added that he needed to let his parents know he was having dinner instead of lunch at our place. I had hoped he would say something more, but he was always clueless. He did everything in a certain way, like an obedient but boring little boy.

"By the way, have you talked to her about the money?"

Over the phone, I couldn't see Zhuoran's expression, but I started to have mixed feelings. It wasn't a good thing, but not an awful thing either.

"Qingqing, if you don't have the money, I can give it to you. Just say that your mom gave it to me. That way my mom would feel better. If she feels that she has been given face, maybe she will like you better," Zhuoran went on to say.

But on this, Zhuoran shouldn't have blamed me. I had been looking for a chance to broach this topic, but for whatever reason, I always choked back my words. The only two members of the family, Mom and I were like creatures from two different planets, each travelling on her own orbit and only looking out for the other in the rarest moments. I never had to report the details of many things to her, or discuss with her, or ask for her advice. And she left me alone most of the time. But this seemed to contradict the perception of Zhuoran's family or that of a normal family.

Actually without Mom's knowledge, I had been to Zhuoran's place to eat twice. His family liked to spell things out up front, typical of Shanghainese families. A bit tough, but at least not hypocritical. But from beginning to end, his mom didn't speak a single word to me. His dad was kinder and asked me about my family.

"Why don't you let Zhuoran visit your place?" asked his dad.

"What's the point?" I thought to myself.

"Next time," I said instead.

"The thing is ..." His dad looked at the chopsticks in my hand before going on: "Even if you live in a shack, you should still take Zhuoran there."

It was then that I realized there was a pair of serving chopsticks beside each of the dishes on their table.

## 2

"What kind of friend is coming?" Mom asked me.

"Boyfriend," I replied.

I was cleaning the dining table with Mom. She popped that question, and was a little stunned hearing my reply. Then she asked: "Oh, so why is he coming to our place? Marrying into our family?"

"Not really," I laughed. "Actually I have no idea. Maybe just for fun."

Mom gave me a poignant look, a little naughty and light-hearted: "No wonder you don't want anything to do with me recently. So you are getting married!"

"No, no!" I hastened to explain. "Don't get carried away. We are not there yet ..."

"It's a good thing even if you are getting there soon." She went back to the kitchen, leaving me to clean up the table and looking as if she had recovered from hearing my news. I was put at ease, at least for that moment. I met Zhuoran at high school. We were secretive at first, then grew comfortable, and then became anxious before melancholy set in because all sorts of tedious things began to torment us. I never tried to share with Mom the worries and grievances throughout it all, and I wouldn't have known how. But I knew that whatever my decision, Mom would respect it. She only wanted me to be happy.

"Qingqing, looks like we should start preparing. Well, since your friend is coming, shall we go to the shop and ask Uncle Lin to take a picture of the two of you?" Mom carried a plate of diced apple into the living room.

"Wedding picture?" I teased.

"No, no!" She hastened to explain too. "It won't be good enough as a wedding picture. Your Uncle Lin has just a small shop and won't be taken seriously. But the truth is that none of those fancy-named photo places out there can take as good pictures as your Uncle Lin. He is still using film which shows some real and difficult skills. His pictures have layers. Young people like you won't get it anyway."

"Mom, can you give Zhuoran two thousand yuan?" I mustered enough courage to ask.

"Ah? But why?" She was taken aback.

Actually I didn't know why either.

"Perhaps, he will be pleased, because it shows that you like him." I tried to remain calm.

"I haven't met him yet, how can I tell if I like him or not. You were just saying not to get carried away by his coming."

"Qingqing, what is it? Tell Mom." Mom suddenly became nervous, which inexplicably evoked in me the same emotion.

"Are you already ..." she pressed on, like Mei Shiping in *The Thunderstorm*. And that scared me.

"What are you talking about. Of course not. You don't have to give him the money, I was just kidding. I know that you won't, and I don't see the point myself. Giving money is the most pointless. But I am caught in between, Mom, and it's really bugging me." For some reason, I got worked up saying all that. But I knew that getting worked up would do no one any good. So I turned around and went back to my room without another word to her. At that moment, I had the urge to cry, but I immediately suppressed it. What's the use of crying.

She knew better than to look for me that night. Everything went back to normal and we went back to our separate planets and our own worries.

# 3

I woke up the next morning to see an envelope on the table with two thousand yuan stuffed inside. It felt heavy in my hand. "Mom has money" was painstakingly written on the note underneath the envelope, which struck a nerve deep inside me. I actually had money myself, and Zhuoran had money too, a lot of money. But he insisted that these two thousand yuan would have an irreplaceable significance for me and for his mom. I thought about it and decided to put the money back in Mom's drawer.

Zhuoran arrived in the evening, holding a shopping bag from Orient Shopping Center. I asked him what was in it and he said: "Cashmere sweater, my mom bought it for three thousand yuan, at half price."

"Nothing for my dad? That's pretty convenient for you."

He looked a little embarrassed and fumbled for words: "I understand he is not with you."

"He is still my dad and not yet dead," I shot back.

"Right, right, I will make up for it later. Don't be mad … Here I am at your place, you should be happy," Zhuoran tried to laugh it off.

Happy.

It's true that I hadn't been happy for a long time and had always been weighed down by one thing or another. While Zhuoran was checking out our place, I poured him a cup of hot water. I was going to turn on the heat, but didn't want to bother to find the control. He coughed a bit and I pretended not to hear. He wasn't that fragile and wouldn't freeze to death. I didn't want to go to any extra length for him, nor did I want to give him money or even heat. Seeing how he was a little shaky drinking the water, I gave him a hot water bottle, saying: "This is how I keep warm."

"Thanks," he said politely with an uncertain glance at me. I didn't remember him being polite for a long while, so I softened when he thanked me.

Zhuoran and I stood at the door together to greet Mom, which took her by surprise.

"Sit, sit, go sit," she let the words roll out without raising her head. That gave Zhuoran pause before he cracked up. I guessed Mom was the one being shy, since I had never brought a boyfriend home before.

"Someone else is joining us for dinner. I bought a lot of stuff," Mom said.

Someone else, I thought. This was new.

"Who?" Zhuoran asked.

I actually had no idea either. Zhuoran paced around, leaving through my books absent-mindedly. He took a closer look at our furniture and pictures on display, the majority of which were of a younger Mom. There wasn't a single picture of me. The old family pictures seemed to have one extra person which we did our best to avoid. In pictures of me together with Mom, I inevitably looked wane and dull next to a vibrant her. So it was that only pictures of Mom's younger days adorned our place.

Mom enlisted my help with washing the vegetables. I washed the green onion and peeled the ginger and asked exactly who was coming.

Mom said mysteriously: "A pigeon walked past our photo shop this afternoon. It was real funny. It stood as if stunned in front of the shop, thought about it for a long time, took a couple of steps forward, went back, then took another couple of steps ... It finally came in. I figured it must be exhausted and couldn't fly anymore, so I caught it and tied its feet. Your Uncle Lin is coming in the evening to kill it, since you also have friend here for dinner." She was very satisfied with herself, as if she had won a war. That poor pigeon was thrown into the basin with feet still tied.

"I like eating pigeons too," Zhuoran cut in.

"Pigeons taste better if steamed with scallops, Chinese Angelica and dangshen," he added.

# 4

Pushing open the door, Uncle Lin looked ready for action, which startled me. Seeing me, he broke into a smile: "Qingqing, where is the pigeon?" Zhuoran laughed at that. "This guy is murderous," he must be thinking.

"In the kitchen. I don't even dare to look. Are you gonna kill it now?" I asked.

"Yes. I will bring it out to say bye to you, ha. Oh, this must be Zhuoran?"

So I hadn't expected that Zhuoran would get to meet Uncle Lin the very first time he came to our place. I had planned to tell him about Lin later and delay his reporting back to his family. Uncle Lin owned the photo shop where Mom worked, and I believed that he would be her last photographer, which should have been perfect. I actually had known Uncle Lin for a long time. To be exact, before my dad left us, we had met at my grandpa's funeral. Mom brought him to take pictures of us and he smiled at me while directing his lens. I couldn't see his eyes but found his smile threatening. And what with the funeral music, an unnamable fear crept up on me.

He wasn't a bad person. Had it not been his existence that spelt the end for my dad, I would have felt that he was the best middle-aged man in the world.

Zhuoran was a little flustered at the unexpectedness of it all, but showed a curious excitement at the same time. I hated this kind of excitement, because it brought out the best side of him for me at a time when I had to disclose that which I felt least inclined to disclose. But maybe marriage was like that. Instead of the luxury for secrets, it was just two people naked in front of each other, proffering imperfection for understanding, and glaring defects too.

Uncle Lin took the pigeon to the courtyard and untied the rope. It collapsed onto the ground, with no strength to struggle at all.

"Feed it something," I said, "Poor thing, and it is good-looking, too."

"You wouldn't have cared if it weren't good-looking, right? It's just a pigeon, and eating it is good for the body," Zhuoran said.

"Don't tell me you haven't had enough scallops, Chinese Angelica and dangshen. This is a life here, and it hasn't done anything wrong!" My temper flared.

Zhuoran stared at me. Without a word, he hooked his fingers into mine, and my heart almost melted at that. I wasn't really mad at him, I was just anxious, nervous, or rather uneasy. He was innocent, too. Who wasn't.

"It's a messenger pigeon," said Uncle Lin. "There was handwriting on the feet. It must have flown a long way. A good pigeon."

We could already smell cooking from the kitchen. Mom seemed to have started cooking her signature stewed eggplant and yellow fish in brown sauce. The rich soy sauce smell almost evoked my childhood memories. There hadn't been so much going on at our place for a long time. I felt like in a dream that I could revisit and move forward from. A beautiful family of four, and everyday family fun.

"Uncle Lin," I said. "Let it go."

# 5

It's apparent that Mom was nervous about the dinner and had no speech prepared. Maybe it was just an impromptu thing, her bringing Uncle Lin back, but it had put me in a difficult position. Uncle Lin secured the pigeon in the courtyard, and the boisterous cooing sounds it made pecking at rice and drinking water punctuated our soy sauce flavored dinner. Mom wouldn't let it go and kept asking "Why can't we eat a perfectly good pigeon." Zhuoran answered by saying that I had a good heart, but the compliment sounded hollow.

Uncle Lin said to Zhuoran: "Qingqing has a bad temper, and you never know which way the wind blows with her. But she has a heart of gold, and I have known her since she was little. She is too sensitive, you will have to accept that."

Zhuoran kept nodding, and Mom nodded alongside.

Mom asked Zhuoran: "How's the food?" and used her own chopsticks to serve him more food.

I tried to stop her: "He can get it himself, no need to help him."

"It's ok," Zhuoran said politely.

People who use serving chopsticks are annoying, I thought to myself.

"Is it good?" I asked instead.

But Zhuoran's reply wasn't important to me at all.

"Uncle Lin is a nice person and we have been friends forever. You need to be nice to Uncle Lin, too," I said coldly to Zhuoran without raising my eyes to catch his expression.

It was getting late. Mom was cleaning up and dicing fruits. I watched TV and played poker with Zhuoran and Uncle Lin. I had never expected the three of us to sit together, in such harmony and warmth and for so much fun. Those were rare moments that felt almost unreal. But for some reason, I had the premonition that it was the first time, and only time. Perfection always came with a darker side and was fleeting.

"I feel old looking at young people like you," Uncle Lin said. "You still have your youth and your life ahead of you, everything is good."

"Uncle Lin, how old are you?" Zhuoran asked.

"This year is my year and Qingqing's year too, so I am ... twelve years older," Uncle Lin took his time to reply.

"Ha ..."

"Twenty-four years older," I corrected him.

"Right right right, I got it wrong. I am getting old and confused," Uncle Lin laughed. Mom seemed to have overheard us and bustled in. She poked at Uncle Lin's shoulder with a wet finger.

"Oh, there's one thing," Uncle Lin looked at Mom and looked at us apologetically, before saying to Zhuoran: "Qingqing is the only child to her mom, I have no kids and have always treated Qingqing as my own daughter. What her mom was trying to say is ..."

# 6

That messenger pigeon stayed with us for quite a few days. Uncle Lin made numerous calls to the Association for Messenger Pigeons but failed to find anyone willing to adopt it. Those who raised pigeons found all sorts of reasons to say no when we offered to give them the pigeon. Maybe they worried about being extorted by us. Neighbors frequenting the photo shop expressed doubt at our wish to give away the pigeon. Someone offered to buy it for food, but was turned down by Uncle Lin. In the end, he decided to keep the pigeon himself, maybe just to please me. I had it figured out and felt bittersweet. He made a special run to the pets market to buy a huge pigeon cage. On the very day he settled down for co-habitation with the pigeon, someone called asking for adoption.

Uncle Lin asked my opinion through Mom, and I said: "Just give it to that person." So the pigeon cage was brought back to our place and left empty in the courtyard where good times were had, or maybe just dreamt about.

Neither of us mentioned again the heated argument that followed that night.

Mom had planned to move in with Uncle Lin so that I could sell our place and buy a new one with Zhuoran. Zhuoran wanted us to live with his family while using my Mom's place as dowry, which was also what his parents wanted. I wanted to stay where my dad had once lived, even if just for one more day.

Zhuoran's dad said to me on the phone: "I had thought you would cherish the chance of marrying into our family, what with your background." At that moment, I felt that I still had a shot at protecting my own family, the same way Zhuoran's family was protecting him.

Mom said to me: "Except for these, I really don't have much for you. I owe you and owe your dad. But I don't want you to look down on yourself, because we all love you. You need to be with someone who likes you, and it has nothing to do with money or house. You will have all of those things later yourself."

"You also need to be with someone who likes you, not for me, but for you," I said to Mom.

"Qingqing, Mom has money," she added after being lost in her own thoughts for a bit.

But those were the last three words that I wanted to hear. I felt that they were the most jarring and hurting three words in the world. Every time she said those three words, I was compelled to give up my life all over again, and I despaired of ever finding any new love to heal the old wound in my heart.

After the New Year, Uncle Lin and Mom got their marriage certificate. The heavy snow that day boded well. I called Mom bride in the snow and she rewarded me with a shy and touching smile. I had never seen her so shy before and never seen her smile like this before.

I took their wedding picture for them, at Uncle Lin's photo shop. The three of us set up and adjusted the lighting together.

I played the legendary photographer in those ancient movies, ordering them to "move to the left, move to the right, move closer and smile!"

And I used film, which showed real skill. I moved around the pictures on the wall at our place to make room for that wedding picture, and realized there was no more room on the wall for the picture of yet one more couple.

At least it snowed. So a good year after all.

# No Choosing Today

## 1

On a morning in 1993, I started walking to school alone by crossing East Tianlin Road. That same day, a little blackboard was put up in front of our classroom. It was one of those original blackboards, black and thin, nothing like the high-end boards made of dark green glass today. My name was written in white chalk on the blackboard, alongside other names which would change every day, like "Late for school today: Zheng Xiaojie, Ma Lijun", "Late for school today: Zheng Xiaojie, Liu Qiongqiong" … I seemed to remember also "Late for school tomorrow: Zheng Xiaojie, xxx". So I was given a nickname, the Late Queen.

I wasn't ashamed at all by such a public display of criticism. I wasn't getting up later than usual, not loitering on the way to school. As usual, my eyes shot open at the sound of the alarm and I brushed teeth, ate leftover rice, went out the door into the alley of No. 13 Apartment Complex, passed a Shandong pancake stall, reached Pingchengge Mansion (which cost a jaw-dropping one hundred dollars per square meter, as rumor had it), crossed the street and arrived at the school gates after passing through the wet market, just in time for the bell to finish ringing. If Mom had been willing to ride me to school on her bicycle, I could have arrived five minutes earlier.

Not only was she not willing. She often forgot to wake me up earlier.

Mom stopped riding me to school because she didn't want to run into a certain person. She tied the key to a red rope around my neck and told me to act smart and cross East Tianlin Road with older pedestrians. On the way home every day, a friendly old lady would look at the key around my neck and ask: "Little girl opening the door herself?" And I would proudly reply: "Yeah!"

"So young and already going home by herself. Poor girl," she liked to add. "Want some barbecue pork? Very cheap."

Later I got to see every day that very person Mom was trying to avoid. He had aggressive features, and the lines on his face spread around his nose bridge like fireworks. I didn't like him, because Mom didn't. He had a chubby son who went to first grade downstairs from my classroom, and I knew him from drawing lessons at Little Star, but we weren't close at all. At that time I found this chubby boy a little dumb.

I agreed to the drawing lessons because of a fight between my parents. Dad was carrying me for a walk near Haoqing Library and was persuaded by a good-looking lady into enrolling me in drawing lessons. He came home to a tongue-lashing from Mom. She had no idea of the good-looking lady's role in all of this. She just preferred piano for me and already put a deposit on a piano through someone she knew. A storm ensued which I had to quell by yelling that I wanted both drawing and piano lessons.

So it was that Sunday was totally lost throughout my childhood. Running around for the lessons year after year turned Mom into a cranky volcano beneath her gentle looks, and dangers of eruption were visible only to Dad and me. So my art lessons were guilt-tinted from the very beginning, as if I was trying to fulfill a promise I hadn't quite grasped myself. But as it turned out, Mom had made the correct choice for me. First of all, the jarring reverberations of my piano practice reduced the frequency of loud grownup talk. Secondly, Dad's enrolling me in drawing lessons when he wasn't thinking straight caused Mom some small trouble.

Since making our acquaintance, "that person" insisted on sending his son to the primary school I was in. And Mom decided not to accompany me to school anymore.

I had no idea which day they broke off. But every day "that person" would look at me from a distance and look behind me, expressionless and without any questions for me. I knew that he probably wanted to ask me something, so I grew nervous. The more nervous I was, the less sure I was about my steps. It was always at that point on the clock that I would see him from a distance looking at me. On a 28-inch black bicycle on the path turning left to school, he would take one look at me before riding off. I thought to myself: I am in second grade now, so the staring contest with this guy has at least three more years to go, how horrifying. And the chubby dummy didn't seem to have noticed anything. He would roll of the wicket seat at the back of the big bicycle like a meat ball and roll into school, beating me by a minute and half, and the gates would close on his heels. So I never saw his name on the little blackboard of his class.

But he never got to raise the flag.

My primary school was at the other end of the wet market of No. 11 East Tianlin Road Apartment Complex. A small lot, with small buildings painted red on the outside that resembled shaky preserved tofu. My biggest wish at that time was to be the one from my class to raise the flag, a wish that was granted in no time. Then I had another biggest wish which was to be a cadre in class, and that wish was soon granted, too. A low-level class cadre, I was put in charge of organizing my own team for cleanup day and fetching a bucket of soup from the canteen at lunchtime.

Since all my wishes were granted, I liked my primary school better than my home where no wish would ever come true.

Starting second grade, my biggest wish was to be the host of the school radio station and to play the national anthem and eye exercise audio for the school every day. My friend Qiqi, who lived in the building in front of us, was a high-level cadre in our class and a popular student. She had raised the flag for more than a dozen times, and she really got to touch the rope. At every handover ceremony, the head teacher of the Students' Council would say that it made no difference whether one got to touch the rope, because the red flag with the five stars brought the same glory to everyone. I felt the teacher was speaking directly to my heart and said exactly the right thing to comfort me. As a matter of fact, everyone could walk by to touch that rope after the flag was raised every Monday morning. I touched that rope many more times than Qiqi, even though our glory would have been equal no matter what.

Qiqi and I officially became friends during a trip to the Martyrs' Cemetery in the second semester of second grade. Qiqi had big eyes, thick brows and hair in two tight braids. She ran fast, spoke sweetly, danced well and read well. More important, she lived the same distance from school as I and was never late. I asked her: "How come there weren't many buried in the cemetery?" She replied: "The cemetery was for the martyrs, for those who died building a new China! Do you see more dead people around, or live ones?" I thought, more live people, of course. I then asked: "Were those real people buried underneath the stones?" She replied: "Yes!" And I asked again: "So their blood was used to dye the red flags and red kerchiefs?" She said with conviction: "Yes!" I was taken aback, thinking how much martyrs' blood had gone into dying the kerchiefs for so many school kids. But I didn't think Qiqi would lie to me, so I asked again: "How do you get to be host of the radio station?" Qiqi said: "Just give Teacher Liu a lipstick."

Qiqi took drawing lessons too, but not at the same place as I. She went to the Municipal Children's Activity Center. She said her drawing was on display at the front of the center, with her name written on it "Zhang Yingqi, Age 7". Because of this, every time Mom suggested taking me to the center, I refused to go. I didn't want to look at that drawing. But at the bottom of my heart, I liked Qiqi a lot. I saw her as the best girl in Class 3, Grade 2.

# 2

Going back to No. 14 Apartment Complex every day from school, I saw Qiqi's dad. He opened a deli store right in front of our apartment complex. It was a glass structure, with just a small rectangular window for a scale. Qiqi's dad sat outside the glass structure next to the small window. He held a small wooden box with a sliding cover for cash from the business.

I talked to him every day, but never had the courage to study exactly how much money that little box contained or whether it had more money than what Mom stuffed under the rug. But I had the feeling that Qiqi's family was richer than ours. Her family's entrepreneurship was a new thing, but accepted by the entire Apartment Complex. It even affected the order in my own family. At that time, Mom was still working at the radio plant, and what she did every day was to pretend to look at hair-thin wiring on a white-lit panel before stamping a blue "Inspected". She made eight hundred yuan a month. I visited the plant and saw Mom at the same thing the entire afternoon, and I asked her: "Can you really see clearly without your glasses, Mom?"

"None of your business," she replied. "Girls with big eyes don't like wearing glasses."

Maybe she was right. So I took a careful look at the complicated wiring secured onto green hard panels which supposedly would reach thousands of households. It was around the same time as my waging the psychological war with "that person" that Mom left for a joint venture where her monthly salary was bumped up to two thousand yuan. Everyone was jealous, but she faked indifference: "The old plant wasn't doing well, so I am just trying my luck with the new place." In Shanghai dialect, "joint venture" sounded the same as "box" which in turn reminded me of the wooden block in the hands of Qiqi's dad. Maybe boxes like these represented some kind of fate. At least, our life would change for the better.

But Dad didn't think so. He had been sulking for many days and spending all his time on the Gameboy at home. I had hoped that he would pick me up from school, but he seemed to be always mad at me. It was only twenty minutes before Mom was to get home that he would abandon the Russian Tetris in his hands or the Contra plugged into TV and wet the floor with a soppy mop. The watermarks on the floor would preempt Mom from blaming Dad for sitting around and doing nothing.

Unfortunately, once Mom started working at the "box", she had less chance of coming home to see the watermarks Dad had meticulously deployed. By the time she got back every day, the floor had dried through. Panic would rise in me with the evaporating water. I didn't like Dad putting on a show, but I didn't like Mom working overtime, either. Every day at the same time, Dad would stare into space with me. Hot meal left untouched, we would watch the news and the commentary, and once the weather forecast was over, Dad would tell me in a dark voice to start eating on my own. I pitied him at that moment. I would then start banging on the piano, *ding ding dong*, to drown out his sighs. *Ding ding dong.*

But unlike Grandma, I didn't try to talk him into getting a job. And unlike Grandma, he didn't try to talk me out of sleeping in Mom's bed.

All that endless waiting saw Dad and me watching breathless League A games (which I found out years later to be all rigged) and numerous pop concerts. Dad liked to say that he preferred the Chairman Mao era, a point driven home by his humming some tune from that era. I said that *Legend of the Red Lantern* would be performed at our school, and he asked me to sing something from the show. But the minute I opened my mouth, he doubled over with laughter, saying that I didn't sound like Li Tiemei at all. He said that he would change his name to Jiushan Feng if he ever got to Japan, because he was always given the role of Jiushan when the show was on at the prosthetics plant.

But Jiushan was a bad person. In my heart, only people like "that person" should be called Jiushan, but I couldn't tell Dad this. Since he lost his job, I was always looking for some innocuous openers to talk to him.

## 3

That morning, my mind went blank when I saw "that person" finally approaching me. Even though I had known this day would come sooner or later, I still freaked out when it did come. "That person" wasn't riding his bicycle. After he saw the sweaty chubby boy roll into the gates, I noticed the cell phone the size of a brick in his hand. I suddenly tried to visualize him urinating with one hand holding that black gadget and the other holding his you-know-what. It was so hilarious that when his fireworks-strewn face got closer, all I could think of was the connection between urinating and cell phone. I peed my pants without intending to.

I knew why "that person" dragged me off as soon as he reached me, and I knew he knew that the reason I didn't scream was I had known him de facto for a long time. I noticed his thick arms, and gory scenes started flashing across my mind like in a movie, including Liu Hulan being killed by a guillotine, Dong Cunrui blowing up a bunker and himself, Qiu Shaoyun being burned to death, and worst of all, Lei Feng being crushed to death by a light pole. Their blood ended up dying the red kerchief around my neck, and my blood would probably end up the same way, at which time the key around my neck would be an equal reminder of my glorious demise, and posters of a smiling me with my quotes noted would adorn the hallways of countless high schools and primary schools.

After depositing me among the trees in front of the school,

"that person" kept rubbing his hands. After a long pause, he asked: "Who are you sleeping with at night now?"

"Fendic ..." I answered in a shaky voice.

"What the heck is that?" he sounded a little put out.

"My elephant," I replied.

"Just you and it?" he asked again.

"And Mom."

He thought about it before asking again: "Where does your dad sleep then?"

"Next to Mom!" I pretended that I didn't even have to look for an answer. But I lied.

Then I noticed his expression becoming a little hideous mixed with indecision. He suddenly let go of me and signed for me to get lost before calling after me abruptly: "Your parents are divorcing, do you know that?" I sprinted towards school in my wet pants, but was already too late. And my name was again on a prominent place on the little blackboard that day, as if it had all been my fault.

# 4

I started to detest the chubby boy since that dreamlike morning. I liked to see him run in PE class and found comfort in his almost fainting from the exertion. I even doubted whether there had really been such a morning when I really had some words alone with "that person". But there had been, as my wet pants testified to. That soaked feeling seemed to have lasted throughout my childhood. After I got back, I threw out Fendic who had never slept with me and took out the cotton in its tummy.

I still waited with Dad every day for the water to dry on the floor. When he went to the bathroom, I would make the effort to mop the floor again. Lipsticks and perfumes started appearing on Mom's dresser. When she took me for the first time to the newly built Orient Shopping Center in Xujiahui, I wasn't happy at all.

And KFC failed to cheer me up.

Around Mid-Autumn Festival, I spilled a bucket of soup for the class and lost my cadreship consequently. Qiqi felt bad for me and told me not to worry and that everything would be fine if I gave the teacher a bottle of perfume. I found Qiqi really nice and always enlightening. But since that soaked morning, I was less inclined to take her advice. For the class meeting, she was going to dance *My Homeland* and asked me to join, and I wasn't enthusiastic about it. For no specific reason, or maybe I just put Dad above raising the flag, dying a martyr or getting a cadreship.

I would still pass the deli store opened by Qiqi's dad every day. But since that day, Qiqi's dad seemed to be extra considerate towards me. He would often give me some deli meat wrapped in grease paper, and the old lady across from his store would often sell me three barbecue sticks and charge me for only two. I was grateful to them, but also wanted so much to kick away the wooden boxes in their hands.

Thanks to Qiqi's recommendation, I became a proud true flag raiser who got to touch the rope. Soon afterwards, I resumed the soup fetching duty. Nothing seemed to have changed and I was back at square one. Or rather everything seemed to have changed inside out and there was no chance of turning back.

When I was about to move up to fourth grade, there was a scandal at school. The son of "that person" was suspected of being mistreated at home, which drew attention from everywhere. I was confused about how he could have been so chubby if he had been mistreated all along. But later the newspaper reported that he had been given a lot of birth control pills which derailed his entire system. Mom read about this in the paper too and commented coldly: "I never liked the drawing lessons. Let's stop them and concentrate on piano from now on."

Dad kept his head bent over the Gameboy, oblivious.

"Did you hear me?" Mom said.

"Yes," I replied.

"Eh," Dad said.

Then he suddenly asked: "Didn't you say that he was a nice person? That his son drew well? That his family was doing really well, what with the cell phone? That you already cut off contact with him? The paper didn't mention the name of the school, so how did you know it was about him and his son and it was the drawing lessons ..."

My heart grew colder with Dad's voice, like the water gradually drying on the floor. The question was whose side I should be on and how I could disappear into the horror like vapor from the floor.

## 5

At the end of fourth grade, Dad asked me who I wanted to live with. I cried. Mom asked me the same question and I cried, too. I wasn't really sad, because I had known about this from the time at the trees. But I couldn't let them know that I hadn't been upset by the knowledge and had had a fulfilling year since. During that year, I lost myself in the national anthem every time I heard it and I was the most enthusiastic about visiting the Martyrs' Cemetery. I had stopped attaching much significance to being a hero, but I would still have liked to die a heroic death. Before dying, I would take out an application to join the Party and hand it to my teary parents: "Please deliver this to the organization. This is my biggest wish. I have another biggest wish, that you won't divorce."

I always remembered how, before he left, Dad asked me for a *Xin Hua Dictionary*. He took his suitcase to the door, then suddenly doubled back. Carrying me to the edge of the bed, he took down two dictionaries from the shelf, the 1985 edition in his left hand and the 1992 edition in his right. He asked me which one I wanted to keep.

"Girl, 1985 was the year you were born, and 1992 was when you were starting school, so Dad bought you this. Tell me, which one you want to keep and Dad will take the other one."

I was really upset looking at his face at that moment. I realized that I would never watch games with him again, or sing, or pretend to mop the floor, all of which was camouflage for waiting for Mom to change her mind and come back to us. I didn't even know where he was going all packed up, or whether he had any plan for getting a job. It wasn't a bad thing, perhaps. I hated it most when classmates asked me what my dad's job was. I didn't like the prosthetics plant which had a funny ring to it, so it's no big deal that he lost his job there and I didn't like him any less for that. But he never asked me any of these. He just repeated his question, whether I liked the red one or the white one, whether the 1985 edition or the 1992 one. Holding up the choosing process, I should really have written my name on a blackboard and hang it in front of our place, in front of school and around my neck:

"No choosing today, Zheng Xiaojie" etc. etc.

# Love

## 1

"How come I can't open it? Can you give it a try?"

The first time I brought a male friend home, I ran into my neighbor Ajin. As soon as she opened her door, her Yorkshire dashed to my side like a rapist and attached itself to my calf. I yelped, although I wasn't really scared, since this had happened before.

"You little naughty! Get back!" Ajin pretended to yell at it as apology to me before carrying it home, without even a glance at me.

"Come on, bro, you can't even get a door open?" I kicked at the iron door and spoke in an unnecessarily loud voice. Iron doors of government housing back then were different from apartment doors. They seemed to invite abuse. Looking fragile and sounding squeaky, they were difficult to open sometimes. They were better defense against the owners than intruders.

I saw incomprehension flicker in Aida's eyes when he heard my words, and the unsteady key paused for half a second in his hand.

"Why did you call me bro?" he looked at me with the unspoken question.

"I don't know. I just panicked." I looked back with the unspoken answer.

Pushing into the door, I caught a glimpse of Ajin looking at us wistfully through the screen window. Turned off by that look, I started banging things around. "Crazy woman," I slammed the door and muttered in a voice loud enough to be heard. It startled Aida again. "Her husband sleeps around and even I caught him at it several times. She is so pissed off that she is acting crazy now, and she looks at people as if they were all having affairs. She thinks she is neighborhood watch or something," I said disgustedly. I found Ajin obnoxious not because she ran into Aida and me, but because she always managed to run into other members of my family. She watched over every single out-of-the-ordinary happening, undisguised. Sometimes I doubted whether this awful antagonism towards her stemmed from my own guilt or her scheming.

While I was closing the door, Aida quickly changed into house shoes like a well-mannered guest. When I turned around, he already took his place in the middle of the living room, his head almost touching the ceiling fan. This was something seldom seen in my family. None of the men Mom went out with was tall, and her life's wish was to marry a long-legged husband. She ended up having to pass down this mission to me.

An indescribable happiness overwhelmed me at the sight of Aida standing timidly under the ceiling fan. His height was a breath of fresh air for my family. It was as if his entrance had put the entire room on alert. I had never had this feeling before, the same feeling as walking into an air-conditioned room to have every cell wake up for the first gulp of fresh air.

Summer was exceptionally early that year. By the time Aida and I reached ground level on a No. 2 Tunnel Line bus, he was clammy all over. I didn't lean on him or say anything important. I had the urge to touch his fingers several times, like in the movies, but suddenly felt that we had all the time in the world for that.

I figured that maybe I should wait till he said he liked me first.

I met Aida when I skipped school which was no big deal at our school. To be exact, I packed up my things and sprinted out the door after catching him leave the room with his schoolbag. I told my desk mate Ashi: "If the teacher asks, say that I went for my injection." Ashi was my best friend and took the fall for me most of the time when I was muddling through high school. But maybe she should hate me, if she still remembered the existence of Aida.

Starting eleventh grade, Aida and I often took the same bus home, but that day was the first time he didn't get off at his stop.

The tunnel we rode through later was built back in 1972. Aida lived on Damuqiao Road and I lived around Yaohua. Before being displaced, mom and I lived on Damuqiao Road too. After that, Aida moved to where we used to live and we moved to the other end of the tunnel. Mom said that a long time ago, soldiers were stationed inside the tunnel to fend off sabotage and a lot of them choked to death on the dust. During my time, I had to go through the tunnel if I needed to go anywhere, but there were no more soldiers to guard the seven or eight minutes' journey in darkness. I had never even seen anyone guard the tunnel at all. So the soldiers became both a legend and a spiritual presence that haunted my childhood with its somberness.

The ride on the dimly-lit bus became unsettling. I was going to tell Aida some of the hearsay, but seeing how he dared not even look at me and took pains to sit a little distance from me, I knew better than to open my mouth. He succeeded in not looking at me and I tried not to look at him. He felt my presence blindly amidst all the noises, and I struggled to read him in silence. This bus ride had remained significant for me ever since. The long dark tunnel, the bus wheels rubbing against the ground, Aida staring straight ahead, and the quietly evaporating sweat, all of these seemed to be scenes from an ostentatious show put on to celebrate the end of my adolescence. Looking back, I didn't think I could ever forget it.

The bus was near empty as it wasn't commuter hour yet. We sat in the sun-baked back and bumped along with the bus. Aida was apparently not used to such bumpy silence, sweat rolling down his neck to seep into his shirt, like right after a basketball game.

"Are we there yet?" he whispered to me.

"Almost," I replied.

A loud bang immediately followed my words and we sprang up and back down on our butts. The sweat at the tip of Aida's hair bounced lightly onto my leg before slipping down to my ankle.

"Actually I have never been to Pudong and won't know how to get back," Aida stammered in a heart-melting attempt at endearing himself to me.

"Same way you came," I thought to myself.

"I will send you," I replied instead, like an understanding older sister. He smiled with relief and held tightly onto my hand, light sweat on his own. This was the first time I held hands with a boy, but he was never my boyfriend.

# 2

"It's so hot. Why are you not wearing shorts?" I asked while fiddling with the A/C remote. It wasn't sensitive or the batteries were eroding. Either way, I struggled for quite a while but still couldn't turn on the A/C. So I had to go back to the room to turn on the floor fan, threw myself onto the floor, and dug out the batteries before putting them back in.

Aida followed me in and carefully checked out my small room. I was a little nervous, but not entirely without confidence.

"Our place is small now, but it hasn't always been like this. My dad had a videogame arcade, but then you know, people like you moved on to Internet bars and he didn't feel like changing. The deal breaker was that he got sick, severely diabetic. So my mom broke up with him. Nothing to be done about it. My mom aims high since she grew up spoiled, not like me. Everyone she dates now is loaded."

"She broke off over some illness?" Aida asked.

"Yeah. Ways of the world, you don't get it? But my dad was lucky and remarried even in his condition. I wonder what the wife saw in him."

"Hey, you don't use A/C often, do you?" Aida suddenly sidetracked.

"Nonsense! We have it on all the time, just that today is the first hot day," I immediately retorted.

"But the plug isn't even in," Aida pointed at the plug hanging below the ceiling while taking a bottle of mineral water from his bag, his clammy Adam's apple wriggling around for a bit.

"Oh, plug it in for me then," I said. "I can't believe that you brought your own mineral water, like a country pumpkin. We should have bought some Kirin before coming in."

Aida dragged over a small stool and stepped onto it only to have his head bump into the ceiling with a bang.

"Ki ... Kirin ... quite ... expensive," the words seemed to be at the tip of his tongue before he bumped his head and he didn't have time to swallow them. "Do you have money?" he asked.

"Not a lot, but some," I answered while opening the fridge to see the green bean slushy Mom left me. I took out two cans of cold beer.

"Zheng Xiaojie," Aida called down to me.

"Eh?" I looked up at him.

"The plug can't go in," he looked at me, embarrassed. Standing up there with hands raised, he looked like a statue.

"Ah well, since it's not too hot anyway." Aida jumped down and moved the stool back.

"You can't seem to do anything right, can't open the door and can't plug in anything," I complained while handing him the beer.

In a small room that didn't really belong to me, I sat down

with Aida who seemed to take up a lot of space. Having nothing to keep ourselves busy anymore, we could only stare at each other, a little uneasy. We were actually not close and could have passed off as strangers at school. Aida wasn't a high profile person in our class and there were many at high school that had no particular character in one's memory. Aida almost became one of them. If Ashi hadn't had a crush on him, I might have had no story to tell about him.

"I don't wear shorts because I have scars on my legs," Aida pulled open the beer can and said slowly.

"That's what I thought. You wore long socks to run in the sports meet." I actually learnt this from Ashi. "I noticed it then," I continued, "Scars are for men. Like in TV, good men all have scars."

"Who exactly?" he asked.

"The Honorable Judge Bao," I thought.

"Xu Yunfeng, who else?" I said instead.

"You know what, I have two scars, too." I peeled back the top of my shorts to reveal a protruding pink mark.

"Two?" he glanced at me while sipping at the beer, as if with disdain. Then he calmly rolled up one leg of his pants.

His long leg was as strong as I had imagined, but was covered with gigantic lines like a map. I sucked in my breath while faking composure. I bet Ashi would have burst into tears at the sight, but I didn't have her deep love for Aida. I liked him of course, just a little bit. But I figured that after me, he could totally pull this move on a lot of girls.

"How ... did this happen?" I swallowed the "wow" that could have been used to convey my astonishment.

"When I was young, I tripped on the wire of a hot pot and got burned," he adjusted his glasses and said matter-of-factly.

"By oil?"

He nodded: "So we have never had hot pot since at home. But my parents are still fighting over this from time to time."

I looked at him and smiled for lack of a better response. I

didn't know how to continue on this track.

"What's your plan after college?" I asked.

"Playing ball, and picking up guitar. And going to Australia with my dad."

"Isn't Australia for retirees? What's the fun," I said disdainfully.

"But my dad said now is the best time to emigrate."

"I see," I said in a low voice, a little deflated.

"You wanna go out to drink after the exams?" I asked again.

"What's the big deal with drinking? I drink everyday."

"Ha, that's good."

Seeing that I was at a loss for words, Aida suddenly said: "When you smile, you look like a gentle girl."

"I am. You are crazy," I gave him the evil eye before bursting out laughing.

"So how come you have scars?" he asked.

"Injections, which led to muscular atrophy, which had to be operated on. They took off some flesh on the left and some on the right, and my butt was one size smaller than others'. The operation room I was in, the kid next to me was having a sixth finger removed, it was so scary. In the same ward there was only one other girl who underwent butt surgery, everyone else was having the sixth finger removed. Doctors didn't even call us by name. I was known as Butt Muscle and the one next to me was Multi Finger, which sounded like some chicken stomach. After my surgery, they didn't even sew me up, but inserted a tube and pressed the blood out everyday without using anesthetics. Whenever the doctor came to press the blood, I would lie on my tummy to watch *Happy Wheel* and my mom would hide in the bathroom."

I burped out the beer in my chest after delivering the speech.

"Did it hurt?" Aida asked.

"I kind of forgot, should have hurt a lot. Has to hurt more than I made it sound," I replied. "What about you? Did you have boils from the oil burn?"

"A lot," Aida replied. "A row of white boils on the legs. Actually I have forgotten too whether it hurt."

The boils were no longer white after deflation. Aida's leg was covered with dark and light brown lines, like rings on a tree or a cake, something that was appetizing.

"Can I touch?" I thought.

"Let me take another look," I said instead.

Aida stretched his long map-like leg to between my legs.

"Hair," I told myself.

"Poor thing," I said instead.

I leaned back on my hands and experienced extreme discomfort. I had the urge to change my position but was frozen by some mysterious force. Through a flimsy veil of unrest, I looked into his eyes and he looked back with even breath.

"There's more up there," he blurted out, pretending nonchalance. But he blushed.

My heart skipped a beat.

Aida then rolled his pants further up, and the map slowly extended further, darker in some spots and lighter in others. It's astounding how injured muscles could heal with such legendary strength. If Aida hadn't been in his prime, or had been skinnier, his leg would have looked like a split branch outside the place I lived.

"Where … does it end?" I asked looking at his leg.

"Right here," he murmured, pointing in a general direction.

In retrospect, I failed to see why I suddenly wanted to touch something in full view. Besides, I didn't seem to have liked Aida that much. At that time, I liked him just a little bit and liked his sexy map-like leg.

The beer cans were dripping water. And my knees felt ice cold when I crawled towards Aida. Because of the sudden change in position, my arms were numb to the point of lifeless. So I had to breathe deep for more strength and extended my fingers gingerly. At that moment, my mind didn't exactly blank out. I suddenly recalled a lyric from singing in the choir, something about "my heart is beating really fast today". What was the song about? Let me think. It seemed to be about Jiang before she died. Excitement overtook me.

# 3

"It's really ... flat." I held my breath and held his eyes, instead of looking closely at the lines weaving through my fingers. "I thought scars would feel uneven," I said, finally taking a breath.

"Ha, what were you thinking, like in a poem, the mountains turning west on top of one another and the trees spreading out towards the north?" My goodness, he sounded like an intoxicated scholar from ancient times, so out of touch and so annoying.

I hated old Chinese most and copied from Ashi for every exam. But I had a stroke of genius and faked ignorance: "What? What turning west? Turning west like this?"

A shocked expression flickered across his brows, then he lowered his head and turned over for half a second to laugh out loud. I had never seen anyone with such an expression before and I didn't think he would ever have the same expression again, so I had a sense of achievement instantly. It wasn't a funny thing in itself, but it cheered me up no end.

"Are you telling me that yours ... aren't flat?" he turned me around to sit in front of him, and his fingers naturally slid across my waist.

"What are you doing?" I slapped his hand off, but didn't say anything to reject him. He then stopped and leaned against the wall peacefully.

"Hey!" I leaned against him.

"Yes?" He didn't exactly hold me. He just poked at my leg erratically at quite some distance from the scar on my butt.

"You look to me like a sexual molester I ran into at Shanghai Book Mall."

"What? What are you talking about ..."

"You know, I went with Ashi to Shanghai Book Mall to buy books ..."

"Buy books? You?"

"Shut up. It's that book ordered by old Chen, who said it would help you advance ..." I slapped his "map" and said indignantly.

"Oh right, so what happened then?"

"So a guy kept pressing against me from behind."

"But I am not pressing against you. Please. You brought me back and sat me down here," Aida proclaimed innocence with a red face.

"Don't get all defensive. I wasn't implying anything."

"Fine," he replied and started to meditate withdrawal like a startled small animal. His calf was stretched stiff as if in a spasm, ice water drops on it. I leaned back to study him and found him a little funny when nervous.

I stood up and straightened my shorts. Then I bent down for a sip of the already lukewarm beer.

"Will you let me kiss it?" I asked tentatively.

"Ah no no!" He immediately tucked in his leg and yelled.

"Not very nice of you, and what are you yelling for?" I asked.

"Cramps ..." With a frown, he held his leg and moaned.

I sat there, laughing till I almost passed out.

"Ah! Your neighbor!" He suddenly slapped at me in astonishment and pointed at the window.

My heart sank and I swerved in that direction.

"Are you nuts? Aida!" I screamed.

# 4

Actually I knew that I couldn't compare with Aida, in many things. Especially after he came to my place that day, especially when he showed me how to pleasure himself. I crouched at the foot of the bed, suddenly feeling sad, a sadness that was seldom seen in my life since I tended to be mindlessly happy. Then I realized I didn't want to like him more, because I didn't think he would be mine and the most we could be were friends a little closer than good friends. And he would never ever be mine, because he was too well-behaved and too good, and we were from two different worlds.

I was a very boring girl, direct, and ready to put up a brave front. I was actually like that for a long time afterwards.

For example, Aida played balls, which I knew nothing about, so I didn't talk sports with him. He played the piano, which I knew nothing about either, so I didn't talk music with him. He had both parents and I didn't quite have both, so I didn't talk family with him. And I learnt from Ashi what he could do and what he had. Ashi could always be counted on to provide me with useful information. But she might never get to know that I once looked at the seldom-shown body of Aida whom she liked most. I would have known more had it not been for the small accident towards the end.

After all, on that day, I did kiss it, not him. That was the first time I took a real look at a man's body. And the beautiful feeling Aida left me wouldn't be diluted by the less than ideal ending of this story.

Because Aida would never push down on my head like on a metronome, or demand that I tilt my scarred butt, or eject onto my face even though the promise was not to. He wouldn't claim to love me while thinking I wasn't good enough, or never kiss me again after pleasuring himself in my mouth. Tedious words like "Sorry", "You will have to excuse me", or "Are you OK?" would never appear in our conversation afterwards, but everyone knew how difficult it was getting nowadays to find a fun and obedient man who would take kindly to "Nuts", "You are crazy" or "Go to hell".

Weird, how come I felt like crying saying all this. Ha.

Anyway, the show Aida put on was hard to forget. He really wanted to be the teacher and I had no idea how to play.

Later, in order to show some sincerity, I told him a top secret. It was before my parents divorced. One night Dad asked Mom: "Can we not have a divorce? We won't have to do that thing till we die, but will you stick with me to the end?"

Mom had no response and turned her back on him. Sleeping next to her, I turned my back on him too. For that, I felt guilty for an entire ten years. He lasted more than ten years, as broken hearts lasted a long time.

I asked: "Do you pity my dad?"

Aida said: "A little, not too much."

I asked: "Why not too much?"

Aida said: "Because I think he can do that thing himself!"

I asked: "How?"

The sun was blazing outside the window and my pulling close the entire curtain didn't help matters. The floor fan squeaked away, but couldn't stop the sweat from popping up on the foreheads of Aida and me, wave after wave. Fortunately Aida forgot about his scarred legs for that moment, although from my crouching position, I saw clearly. He was burned on the entire left leg and upper right leg, and he closed his legs to make a complete pattern. Intimate, mythical and eternal.

Maybe I shouldn't have had such a strange request and he shouldn't have been mad for no reason. Because when he straightened up, his neck and arms were crimson. And his eyes glazed over. I thought he would spit out: "Are you happy now?" But he didn't.

He said: "Zheng Xiaojie, I feel dizzy."

# 5

When Aida said: "Zheng Xiaojie, I feel dizzy." I heard the iron door being kicked in the distance.

"Ajin, are you taking *Nuan Nuan* for a walk? Hi there, you little naughty!" I heard mom's voice.

"I brought Adi here back to help move a fridge, gonna be noisy."

What the heck was Adi?

"Aida, Aida," I pushed at his leg, shoulder and face.

But his whole flushed body was collapsed onto mine.

"Aida, wake up, don't scare me," I was scared witless and tried to hold him up, but he was too big for me. I grabbed a couple of napkins and wiped the white liquid off the floor. Then I tied his pants and wiped the sweat off his face. He struggled to keep his eyes open without making a sound. He seemed to be looking through me with red vicious eyes, but was hanging onto my hands all shaken up.

"Moving fridge, ha, who are you kidding."

I heard a man's voice, damn it, and had to hold my breath.

"What did you expect me to say then, moving a person?"

The front door was then closed, not exactly in a gentle way.

"Aida, listen to me, my mom is back and we have to leave before they get to the living room." I held his face and whispered to him. "I will carry your shoes for you and we will walk barefoot at first. Don't make any sound, do you remember? Can you try standing up on your own? Please try?"

In his half-collapsing state, Aida wasn't such an imposing presence anymore. I opened the door quietly and looked at the wall clock to see that it was approaching four. I would have been back home around quarter to five on a normal day. They were really too much. Thinking about this, I almost cursed out loud.

I carried my own bag and held Aida's in my hand. I put on flip-flops and took Aida's shoes with me. They hadn't even noticed this unfamiliar pair of sneakers. They were totally oblivious.

I closed the door stealthily and out of habit, glanced across to see Ajin staring at me through the screen window. I had no time for her now and couldn't exactly wait for that little womanizer to make another appearance. So I stumbled with Aida outside.

Passing our window, I seemed to hear rustling sounds from inside, and I was a little offended.

"Hello Auntie! Zheng Xiaojie, what are they doing? Ha, ha, ha." He was drunk, scaringly drunk.

I helped Aida to the flower bed and put on his shoes for him.

"Quiet," I said. "And let's go."

# 6

On the No. 2 Tunnel Line bus, Aida leaned all his weight against me, alcohol on his mouth and nostrils smelling as strong as if he had drunk several barrels. In the darkness, I kept my fingers on the five coins left in my pocket as if they were the only funds to save Aida. I even wished the tunnel to be longer and wished that guards would be lined alongside. That way I would know that I was protected.

Rainwater flooding, seawater flooding, come whatever calamity, I didn't find it horrifying at that moment. I suddenly wanted to look for Dad, even though I hadn't seen him for a long time, come to think of it. Since that night when Mom and I turned our backs on him, he completely disappeared from our lives, like the soldiers who had never appeared.

But what should I do? The timing was awkward. School was over and Aida was drunk. Didn't he claim that he drank every day? What bullshit. All men were full of bullshit.

# 7

"Drunk? He is allergic to alcohol! Shoot, you need to go to the hospital. Do you see rash on his arms? But ... how did you two end up together? Did you know each other?"

From the public phone booth in front of Nanyang High School, I summoned Aida's good friend Lin Jun.

# 8

By the time I managed to get home, it was completely dark. I figured that Adi should have left before finding my way home distractedly.

Ajin never bothered with me whenever I opened the door by myself. One of those days I was going to dig out her prying eyes. That tongue-wagging woman.

"What's wrong with you? Getting home so late. Where on earth have you been, and wearing only a tank top. You think it's mid summer? It's only June, silly."

My nose was assaulted by a strong smell of vegetables which made me nauseous. For whatever reason, a few short hours had turned that breath of fresh air in our place into something murky.

"You are back, Jiejie."

I was startled at hearing a man's voice.

"No way," I thought.

"Hi there, Uncle," I said instead.

"Jiejie, I have been so busy after coming back and had no time to put things away, so Uncle cleaned up your room for you. Hurry up and open a beer for Uncle."

Room? Clean up? My goodness ...!

I dashed into the room to see the water mark on the floor gone, and napkins too. I turned around and he was standing behind me, the top of his head reaching only my nose. And he had a bulb for a nose.

"Don't you ever touch my things again!"

I heard Mom dump vegetables into the hot wok, with a jarring sound.

"I won't tell, about the shoes," Bulb Nose smiled at me wickedly which made him look uglier than when he wasn't smiling. I swore I had never seen such an ugly man anywhere before, a man so ugly that I couldn't imagine he had once been young too.

Why didn't Mom turn her back on such a person? Was she

really getting old? Or just confused?

"Go tell, see if I care," I said madly. "Get out!" I yelled.

"And the napkins." He kept his cloying smile.

"Get out!" I yelled louder.

He backed out of my room politely with the ghost of a smile.

This one was even worse than the last one. They were getting worse, I thought. Had I known, I would have behaved and not scared off so many men when I was younger. Too late now. I was too naïve, thinking that I could always trade up when dating. But Mom's experience convinced me that I would only trade down.

# 9

Many years later, when I found Aida and Ashi through the Internet, Aida had settled down in Canberra. This summer he posted pictures of him with bikini-clad girls in Hawaii, him wearing flowery long pants. Ashi got into New York University. I knew that universities named after cities couldn't be too good or too bad either. Like Beijing, Shanghai, Nanjing and New York.

Fortunately Aida didn't run into Bulb Nose that day. And I didn't continue with Aida. We were placed in different classes and he started taking lessons at IELTS. With no specific goal in mind, I joined the decadent liberal arts class. Aida would never know that Bulb Nose did become my stepdad. After they got married, I sometimes found Mom the same short and same obnoxious.

In my junior year in college, Dad passed away. On the day he died, I took my boyfriend on a creaky bus ride to Puxi to see him for one last time. Dad lay in his suit in a transparent coffin, expressionless. His wife read the eulogy, about how he fought in the war to defend the country in his younger days and was scarred all over on his legs, and how he eked out a living from the local gangs after leaving the army to run an arcade. I never knew these things and I wondered how she knew.

"Did you love your dad?" my boyfriend asked me after we got home.

"So so," I replied.

I opened the glass window of his place and closed the screen window. It's a good thing that I would never see Ajin from across again. I should feel grateful that he took me in, or that he loved me, so that even before I finished college, I didn't have to look at Bulb Nose's horrible face day in, day out.

"You know … Before my parents divorced, one night my dad asked my mom: 'Can we not have a divorce? We won't have to do that thing till we die, but will you stick with me to the end?'"

"My mom had no response and turned her back on him. Sleeping next to her, I turned my back on him too. For that, I felt guilty for an entire fifteen years."

I asked: "Do you pity my dad?"

He said: "I pity myself too, and I don't want to be so pathetic!"

I actually had no pity for him at all. He took all my first times as if they were his for the taking, and broke up with me in the end. I couldn't exactly say I wasn't sad. But what's the point of feeling sad.

The last time we made love was the next summer, after we had downed two cans of cold beer and water from the cans had dripped all over the floor.

"How much longer?" I asked in a small voice.

"Almost," he panted.

At that moment I was indeed sad. Because I thought of Aida, and how we watched our adolescence play in front of us on a bumpy ride through a familiar tunnel. That year saw him traversing darkness with me for the first time, and I wasn't sure if we ever saw light.

# Summer Days

## 1

I had never expected to run into Xiaomao at Mountain Lodge, our childhood haven before it was taken over by a Jiangxi cuisine restaurant. Xiangyang Park has been completely transformed into a venue for the middle-aged to dance and make friends, which is quite a spectacle in Shanghai. I didn't know until many years later that the parks and zoos in China are the only ones in the world to open at seven in the morning to welcome aunties and uncles with bouncy steps. It doesn't matter whether their audience is their own selves or peacocks, hippos and elephants.

Young lovers no longer lingered in parks. Our haven, Xiaomao and I, gone without a trace.

The primary school kids who had witnessed the first kiss between Xiaomao and me have disappeared from Xiangyang Park. Come to think of it, they were more hyped than us, running around, screaming and grinning like crazy. Those kids might have all started high school by now and have turned into tormented high school students like we used to be. It was on this way back from school that we literally saw them grow, as if overnight, from kindergarteners carried around like huge meatballs to naughty primary school kids carrying square schoolbags and prequalified for wearing the red kerchief. I have always wondered whether those kids were assaulted by mosquitoes as they stood still to spy on us. It was a scorching summer and the cicadas had cried themselves hoarse. Once I got home after the kissing, I counted more than thirty mosquito bites on my legs. The burning itch overshadowed the sweetness on the lips, and mosquitoes were better kissers than Xiaomao and I. And our kisses after that first time were less patient or oblivious to the buzzing blood suckers. We allowed our sweat to roll down onto each other's face, unthwarted.

And some time later, the scorching summer days came to an end.

The last time I saw Xiaomao was our sophomore year in college. He had just had a heart surgery and sat a little bloated across from me, holding a throw pillow. Back then, a tea house was where Mountain Lodge was. A beeping gadget with turning pages was placed on the marble tabletop for taking orders. A tea house was a relatively grownup place for us. High school kids dating prematurely might meet there to order a cup of hot cocoa for ten yuan which could have bought eight point three barbecue sticks and six point six corn cobs.

The soft sofa was so low as to look collapsed in. Xiaomao's knees peeked above the tabletop, so that sitting there, he could have been mistaken for a basketball player. That, of course, would have been his beloved career. When it came to writing articles, if the theme was an unforgettable thing, he would write about basketball; if the theme was an interesting person, he would write about a basketball player; and if the theme was a group activity, he would write about a basketball game. He would draw a blank if he couldn't relate the writing to basketball. And when the Chinese teacher asked him why, he lifted his head and kept his mouth in an embarrassed O. Sweat popped up on his forehead and rolled along undulating cheeks to his neck, chest and tummy, before he croaked out a "What?"

The Xiaomao in sophomore year behaved the same as in high school, even after a major procedure. He just stared at me. He had recovered sooner than I imagined, and was pale as a marshmallow. But now that I was facing him, I was still a little unsettled and secretly made up my mind to never see him again. I was going to move from Puxi to Pudong, to follow Mom's marriage across the river to a faraway place. And he had just barely beaten death. So it's better not to dwell on the complexity of it all, but start anew instead. And the most important thing was that we had already broken up and I felt guilty about meeting him without telling my boyfriend. If he hadn't been sick, this meeting wouldn't have happened.

After a long silence from me, he suddenly said; "I sneaked out this time. My mom wouldn't have allowed it." Then he laughed with a nutty sense of achievement. So I had to ask how come he sneaked out with a throw pillow and he replied irrelevantly: "Qianqian, they took out my heart this time, fixed it and put it back, so I have one more scar on me now."

Did it hurt? I thought.

"It's good for men to have scars," I tried to brush him off, carefully, speaking as if he had just recovered from a cold.

"Right," he answered in a low voice. "But I can never run again, or play basketball. Ever."

Ever. A word he had never said to me before. We seldom used such extreme wording, but I believed he meant it this time.

Then there's what he wrote: "Qianqian, tell me the truth, are you happy that you broke up with me? This way you won't have to face a disabled me."

He wrote in black and bold, making the words all the scarier.

## 2

Xiaomao was my first boyfriend. I liked him a lot and he liked me back. We went to the same neighborhood high school of the

New Apartment Complexes. He was tall and wore long pants all year long. Whenever there was a group activity requiring shorts, he would refuse while staring everyone down and not bothering with an explanation. I almost believed him to be disabled, like the solider in the movie, who was incredibly handsome and ready to take anyone on, but who revealed a steel rod when rolling up his pants.

He was indeed my Iron Man.

One time I was sprinting to catch a class and ran right into his chest with a solid thud when turning on the stairs. Breath knocked out of me, I looked up at him. He was unfazed and teased me: "Sorry, Yu Xiaoqian, I am Iron Man."

I said "Nuts" to myself while in extreme pain on my head. But strangely, I didn't demand an apology. We were in eleventh grade then, and I wasn't a particularly pretty girl at school and never had my bra straps pulled by male students or sticky cocklebur thrown onto my hair. He didn't stand out, and no one noticed him except when he had to write sorry notes for every time he refused to wear shorts because of the scars on his legs.

Since crashing into him that day, we started having more eye contact. I would leave a can of black tea in a crispy white FamilyMart plastic bag at his desk every morning. He caught on one day. I was leaving the supermarket after having paid, and he stood in front of me, as imposing as a wall. I almost crashed into him again before he moved easily out of the way, pointing at his chest: "It hurts."

Every morning after that, I would buy him a can of black tea and he would buy me a can of cocoa which gave me the urge to run to the bathroom during every first class of that year. One day, he suddenly took a square plastic box out of his blue schoolbag. Inside the box was a 3.5-inch disk on which was written "Information Technology Principles". He gave the box to me with a solemn expression as if we were engaged in undercover work. It was funny.

Xiaomao didn't cross my mind again till 2008, when the blockbuster movie *Iron Man* officially started shooting in the US. I remembered him saying to me: "I can't be your Iron Man anymore, I have a scar here." He pointed at his chest and I didn't know what to say. He removed the throw pillow, peeled back the opening of his T-shirt to reveal a fine scab. Things were becoming advanced and unrecognizable then. N86 computers were replaced by Pentium ones, photos didn't have to be developed from film, music could be downloaded, and sutures for heart surgery were glued instead of embedded. I wasn't quite used to it all.

The truth was that I thought of Xiaomao a lot over the years. Every time I inserted my ATM card, I would be reminded of that disk that almost suffocated me. I couldn't even find a more similar replacement. "I like you", he wrote on the disk, in red and bold. It highlighted what was stored in the black disk, and stood out so vividly in my own memory, indelible like a virus.

Fortunately Pentium finished it off for us, because floppy disks didn't stick around long enough. We spent the money for barbecue sticks and sweet corn on sixteen "Information Technology Principles" disks which had become corpses since.

On the day of the tea house meeting, he handed me the seventeenth 3.5-inch floppy disk with heart-stopping words written inside, in black bold. But I didn't see them on the spot. He said matter-of-factly: "I was going to put some audio on it, but memory was too small and I couldn't have said much." He also gave me a huge gift box and I took it, imagining a life-changing gift. I opened the box to see more than five hundred FamilyMart plastic bags that once contained the black tea I bought him and the cocoa he bought me. Used only once, they were still crispy and folded neatly to resemble library cards from old times.

If I was honest with myself, I have never seen anything more like love than those plastic bags over the years. But I replied in my heart: "Too late, because I am with another person, and we already travelled together." It was something fancier than going to a tea house, something irreversible. There was a hole in my body too, and I had also been damaged.

So even when the white plastic bags struck the deepest chord inside me, bags that were so neat as if they had been ironed over, I had to convince myself that I didn't love Xiaomao anymore.

I couldn't face him anymore.

I hadn't had a good time since leaving him. The several relationships I had had were all lost to inflation and skyrocketing housing prices. With my sensitiveness and smarts, once a relationship got past superficial flirting, the end was near. Whenever I was in a jam, I thought of Xiaomao whom I couldn't get hold of anymore. I would estimate his age and imagine his job. And when I had a suitor, I would visualize in broad strokes Xiaomao's then girlfriend, whether she was seemly or plump, or whether he was unfortunate enough to fall in love with an Amazon woman.

I wondered what it felt like making love to someone with weird-looking scars all over his body. But it had to be totally different from sex with a flabby-tummy teenager, a beer-belly older guy, a tattooed hooligan or a bespectacled science nerd. It was all just off the top of my head.

I experienced an emergency landing after a thunderstorm on a flight to Taipei. I could see lightning and thunder outside the window, but couldn't register anything horrifying in my ears. I seemed to have felt the presence of death, dancing next to me or ushering in the inevitable. I saw myself as a peacock, hippo or elephant at the Shanghai Zoo forced to watch *Ode to Heroes* performed by dancing elderly women, and I forced myself to concentrate on death and risks.

When Xiaomao's heart was being patched up, it might have looked like the brilliant thunderstorm seen from inside the cabin, so quiet, so gory and so pressing. Bodily pains and marriage risks lost all significance at that one moment. Already at a child-bearing age, I imagined how happy I would have been to have a son like Xiaomao. I would never abandon him to fighting death alone. But unfortunately I would never have the chance to confess how naive I had been to panic and run off.

I was shaken to the core inside the violently shaking cabin, powerless. My cup shot up in front of me onto the floor. All I could think of was Xiaomao's heart with the hole in it. But come to think of it, I should have been the one abandoned, hole-riddled.

# 3

So when I saw that familiar figure cuddling with a girl at a corner of Mountain Lodge, I was shot through the heart. I first saw their four legs, Xiaomao's clad in pants, of course. I never got to see inside the pants. I ran off before I had the chance.

Maybe she had got to see.

I was just speculating. The four legs were so close together, and the mere inches in between were lovers' space. They didn't sit any closer, but no one could have outdone such a public display of intimacy. I hesitated for a minute and half about whether to go over and say hi. It had been six years since last time, after all.

Xiaomao and that girl cuddled at the corner of Mountain Lodge, seemingly staring at some app that needed full concentration on the iPad. Their leaning against each other to do the same thing felt alien to me. Xiaomao's fingers would slide across the touch screen, and her fingers would take over sometimes. They looked serious and unwilling to give up their turn with the screen.

He had gained weight. His shoulders were still the same broad, but thicker and less Iron Man-looking. Maybe it was because of lack of exercises. I was reminded of that saddening "ever", a six-year long "ever" that had gone by just like that.

I didn't have an iPad, and I broke up with Xiaomao once

the memory of the disks exceeded 128M. So we seldom stared at the same object like he was doing with that girl, except when we were copying homework together. Every night during high school, whenever I opened my homework, I would turn on my blue screen cell phone. My dad gave it to me, not a name brand. It was the only gift from him my entire life and cost him six months' child support, which my mom berated him for. I knew that it was a bargain purchase and difficult to use. Its only contribution was to connect me and Xiaomao in our love.

Xiaomao texted me one day that he wouldn't be able to see me in the morning for a whole week because he had to see a doctor.

"I have a hole in my heart from when I was a kid," he wrote. "Don't worry, I am Iron Man."

I recalled that sunken spot on his forehead that looked out of place. I was told that it was the result of frequent IVs for his heart defect when he was a kid and couldn't be smoothed over after one year's rubbing ginger over it. I had noticed that spot when I crashed into the Iron Man. It must have been after I received that text that I started loving him a little less. I had all my sensors out for the connection between disease and love on TV and in the papers. I even wanted to save money for a new heart for him, but gave up such impossible thoughts when my mom ridiculed me for failing to reach my dad after six months' calling his number.

"It has been a while, Huang Xiaomao. I just got back from a business trip to Taipei. Fancy running into you here," I walked to him while trying to suppress the blood gushing to my head.

An indescribable panic flickered in Xiaomao's eyes, and his mouth opened to an O without making any sound. I didn't read any love or hate or forgotten-ness on his slightly chubby face. All I could see was defeat. He looked like an empty file gaping at me, waiting for my notes and confessions to reveal to him what we had both gone through over the years.

He still said nothing and just looked at me.

"It has become a restaurant here. I am meeting a friend, then I saw you. So long then, enjoy your meal," I added.

I actually didn't see that girl's face. She never lifted her head to look at me, so I couldn't have taken a look at her. I was embarrassed by Xiaomao's silence, however. We stared at each other for a couple of seconds and I decided to back off, since he hadn't said anything offensive, like all those people I met afterwards.

They would probably marry soon, I thought suddenly as I turned around. That's good, better than where I was. Xiaomao looked good. He hadn't died a sudden death or been weakened. Xiaomao was such a nice person. He still remembered this place and remembered to bring girls here. He hadn't changed a bit and still wore long pants on a scorching day. He was still enthusiastic about electronics and about playing games for his girlfriend. The game he was playing for me on my blue screen cell phone was frozen where he had left it, and the phone was laid to rest in my drawer with all those floppy disks.

# 4

When I was finally summoned to the private room by non-stop urgent calls, I had none of the previous indecision, sentimentality and confusion. I suddenly realized that Xiaomao might have forgotten me and forgotten how I had hurt him by abandoning him. In fact, I might have been the only one drowning in my guilt and failing to see a plausible way out all those years.

"Miss Yu, being late isn't a good habit, you know."

The guy didn't look young. According to my mom, he was a typical man from Zhangjiang, simple-minded, smart and rich, whose parents were both government employees. "What better person do you want?" she said this every time, sad and despairing.

"Miss Yu," the man from Zhangjiang piped up. "I waited an entire twenty minutes for you, and I went to all the trouble to find a place with easy parking."

"I wasn't late," I was offended for no reason.

"And I have no car!" I added.

"That so. How come my mom said you have a car? What other fake data do you have? I was given to understand that you were born in 1986, graduated from East China Normal University, make six thousand yuan a month, have a car, have a one-bedroom place mortgage-free, no medical history, divorced parents, remarried mom who lives with you, three previous relationships and you refused to disclose whether you are still a virgin ..." I raised my eyes to look at him, and he didn't seem to be joking or venting. He just looked at me, dead serious, then looked at his iPhone.

"Anything to drink?" I asked.

"What would you like to drink?"

"Black tea from a can," I replied.

"I am sorry, Miss. Here we only have Jupu, Longjing, Tieguanyin and Jasmine ..." the waitress joined the party.

"From here, turn left to Xiangyang Park, go through the flower garden of the park, there's a FamilyMart where ..." I answered.

"Jupu," the man from Zhangjiang said firmly.

I experienced a sudden happiness as soon as I sat down in the private room. Mountain Lodge lived up to its name. I had more than one mosquito bite within just a few minutes. These mosquitoes seemed to have come to my defense when I found myself in a difficult situation. They urged me to continue fighting and not to be afraid, and they reminded me that some life-turning events were granted extra significance only by life's own logic.

"Miss Yu, what kind of man do you like?" he asked as if reading from a script.

"Iron Man!" I said cheerfully.

"Miss Yu, my mom told me that you like computer guys. I am very confident about my profession. What kind of computer work do you have in mind?"

"Floppy disks," I replied.

"Miss Yu, you must be a humorous person. Floppy disks have long been phased out ..."

Phased out, I thought to myself. What a scorching summer. The cicadas have cried themselves hoarse.

# Memory Is the Slowest

## 1

"I can't ever sleep well again," Xia Bingbing thought while straining to pick up the kettle from the stove and pour the boiled water into the bottle. She was a little unsteady and her feet felt like giving away. The steam from the bottle opening turned her fingers as pink as peeled mice. She had brought the kettle from her hometown more than a decade ago. It was called copper pot in Shanghai dialect, which was quite befitting, since it looked yellowish. The crevices were all stained blackish yellow and a metal scrub had left uneven scratch marks on the outmost rim. Xia Bingbing hated most the sound of metal scrub over copper kettle, and the mere thought of it electrified her scalp. The aged screen window at Uncle Zhou's place faced the stove and was stained the same blackish yellow. Intuitively Xia Bingbing averted her eyes from such an unseemly sight. She turned around and made ginseng tea for Uncle Zhou before pouring water into the basin to wash her face.

How did it get so hot overnight? And the heat persisted into the night. Xia Binging didn't believe any one of them was capable of sound sleep, even though no one got up in the middle of the night. They just carefully and stubbornly sucked it up. The ceiling fan squeaked away, indifferent to the dust that refused to detach itself. It started to get light really early, and for Xia Bingbing, watching the sun rise was the most despairing. The fresh and vibrant sense of loss tore her apart more than the loneliness at night. She wanted desperately to get used to it all, and to not be emotional about everything. But she had just grown familiar with it and had never contemplated extracting herself.

Even on a hot day, Xia Bingbing liked washing her face with hot water. She buried her face in the steam and breathed with difficulty in the enveloping warmth. Having nothing to be sad about, she still got teary momentarily.

Zhou Lei was already not living at home then.

It's always easier for the one leaving first. Of the four of them, he got out the earliest. For whatever reason, after he left, Xia Bingbing felt more at ease, even though she hadn't wanted him to leave. Uncle Zhou sold the sofa after he left, since he had been tricked into buying it in the first place, when he was poking his nose into others' business. For that he had a fight with Bingbing's mom. He hadn't really done that much wrong, as a matter of fact, except that he failed to be fair when dividing things up. So through no fault of his own, Zhou Lei ended up sleeping on the crappy sofa for seven, eight years. There just wasn't enough living space, and there was no privacy for anyone to misbehave. So everyone abandoned all secrecy and privacy. After Zhou Lei left, Xia Bingbing naturally became a little careless, and she didn't mind as much when Uncle Zhou nagged: "You need two cloths for washing dishes, who do you think we are?" Nagging as he was, Uncle Zhou had become more cheerful after Zhou Lei made room for everyone and teased her in small dirty ways from time to time, which was better than her glum mom. He was confident that he could read Xia Bingbing and control her, although he had no real intention of bullying her. All he wanted was to get something more out of her dad, which her mom had no problem with. Not having seen her dad for more than a decade, her mom wouldn't lose sleep over such a person from her past, although she never lost sleep over Xia Bingbing either. But Zhou Lei's abandoning ship played right into her hands. Xia Bingbing hadn't seen her in such a good mood for a long while.

Xia Bingbing loved the sight of Uncle Zhou coming home after being shortchanged outside. It's strange that all these years later, he still couldn't act or even pretend. He had a stunned look, but would flare up whenever asked a question and start acting passive aggressive. It was hilarious and attractive for her mom, as Xia Bingbing well knew. Zhou Lei couldn't stand his passive aggressiveness either, but never bothered to reason with him. It's conceivable that they were never meant to get along, and Uncle Zhou was never meant to listen to reason, even though you might have rehearsed hundreds of speeches in your heart. To quote Bingbing's mom, he was a rascal, and there's nothing you could do about his plopping down on his knees and pleading with you in tears. You had to back off, and he figured he had won by dint of his rhetoric and moves.

After getting up and before brushing his teeth, Uncle Zhou made a greasy appearance at the stove, sipped at the tea Xia Bingbing had made for him, and asked smilingly: "Hey Bingbing, did you sleep well last night? So hot, isn't it?" And Xia Bingbing smiled back, dry and cold: "Uncle, what do you want for breakfast?"

"I want salty pastry. Two, and salty soybean milk."

"What about Mom?"

"You know what? I actually want something sweet. So get sweet pastry and sweet soybean milk."

"What about Mom?"

"Get a salty one for her, we can share."

## 2

Her mom got up late every day, but she did get a lot done once she was up. She was just not an early bird by habit, because she couldn't sleep well. So mornings truly belonged to Xia Bingbing. She would take her time going out to buy breakfast every day, hoping that by the time she got back, the other two were already looking decent. The humid heat at night was a torture, but she wasn't alone, because the two people lying close to her were tortured as well. They were waiting for the others to fall asleep first. It's a tacit understanding that they would watch out for each other's movements, and even the smallest sounds were full of possibilities. But of course, some desires were hard to catch just by listening. At times like this, Xia Binging wanted so much to move out, like Zhou Lei did.

But Zhou Lei didn't get to move out just because of this. He had to first give up the subsidy his mom left him. His mom was an overseas Chinese who had seen better days. Uncle Zhou took her in for a while and had Zhou Lei with her. She had gone back to her own country and left them the crappy place they were living in. The poor nowadays could strike rich if the government wanted to take back their housing, so Zhou Lei had kept his residence registration with them and agreed to forfeit his claim to whatever new housing they might be assigned by the government.

Her mom had everything of hers, so Xia Bingbing had nothing to leave behind and was relatively free. But she didn't know where to go. She gave it some thought and figured that with nothing to her name, a new life had to come from her own self or a man. These were the only two options, but the first one seemed too difficult. As for the second one, she already … This was where dissatisfaction set in.

By the time she got home with pastry and soybean milk, her mom was up. Refreshed, she demanded loudly: "Girl, what took you so long? You came back so late, I am starving." Her forehead was covered with as much sweat as Xia Bingbing's, and she already changed into an embroidered silk dress which showed every contour of her body.

She took a piece of pastry and dragged herself back into the room.

"How could you take my sweet pastry?"

"What the hell, you grudge me even some pastry? Be more generous like I am to you."

"Ok ok, I just meant that sweet is good, sweet is good, like butter in honey, butter in honey."

Xia Binging turned on the faucet to wash her face, the water almost sun-baked warm. Today was turning into a scorching day, the heat already buzzing so early in the morning. She sighed gently, thinking that she still had to go out today which sucked.

Uncle Zhou came out to get his sweet soybean milk. Soon afterwards he was ready for work, a plastic bag around his wrist. Xia Bingbing was going to go into the room, but he doubled back to fetch the tea she had made for him.

"What are you doing in the kitchen, Bingbing? Not feeling well?"

"Not too bad," Xia Bingbing smiled drily. She regretted saying it immediately and wanted to add: "A little … hot."

"Come on, girl, you weren't knocked up, were you?" Xia Bingbing was taken aback, but the feeble resentment soon evaporated. She just stared at him, disgusted.

Uncle Zhou sidled past her: "Uncle Zhou knows!" He grinned at her before saying in a self-congratulatory tone: "I am off to enjoy my A/C!"

Uncle Zhou had been working as a security guard at the print research institute next door since his retirement.


# 3


Xia Bingbing went inside to see that her mom had already laid out her clothes for going out. T-shirt and shorts that she had worn six years ago to attend the professional school.

"Mom, I have no shoes to go with these. I can't wear my white slippers or the blue ones."

"It's always one thing or another with you. I got you shoes already."

Xia Bingbing glanced under the bed and saw a pair of sneakers with light green pattern and white soles. Where had she dug them out from?

"Mom, they said to wear black."

"To hell with black. I found something red, from a long time ago, too. But you have boobs now and it won't fit. What do you want to dress up for? If they see that you are having a good life, they will gang up on you. I told you, I will never have anything to do with them, except for one thing, that you pay respect to the dead, you know? You are not young anymore, and you should know who is the one taking care of you all these years. Just that the old woman was really vicious and had to pick such a hot day to die, was she trying to drag everyone down with her? Anyway, just go, take an umbrella, you will have to change buses, it's so far ... and make sure that you eat before coming back!"

Under a blazing sun, Xia Bingbing set out. She took the same route when her grandpa passed away the first half of that year, so she knew where she was going. This old couple chose to depart within the same year, one in the freezing winter, the other in the scorching summer. But compared to when her grandpa died, Xia Bingbing was a little sad this time. Within six short months, it was her dad's girlfriend instead of her dad who notified her of the funeral. That woman with a cloyingly sweet voice sobbed over the phone and kept saying what a poor thing Grandma was, and asked her to accompany her to the funeral since her dad wasn't home.

This whole thing was the showiest kind of show for her mom, no doubt about it. She spent the whole evening bombarding the woman whom no one had ever met, and at midnight, she slapped away Uncle Zhou's groping meaty hand. Xia Bingbing heard clearly.

Her dad and her mom were actually alike in that, Xia Bingbing thought. Too bad that she was too insignificant to tip the balance against that one in bed. She got it, but she still couldn't help feeling sad that someone outside the family had to call her up and tell her. Maybe someone that wasn't family would bring all her family news from now on.

It was a sizable funeral and those present were bubbly and chatting as if attending a gathering that didn't happen often. Her grandma snickered at everyone from her picture in the distance. She didn't have a kind face to begin with, and she couldn't recall all the kids' names out of real confusion or fake one. Her long-standing justification was: "I did my job giving birth to all of you." So her descendants were scattered everywhere and didn't really get along. The Xia family did well with reproduction and there were more than twenty in Xia Bingbing's generation, but they seldom saw each other because of broken families, and she had only vague impressions of them from childhood. The uncles and aunties that she could still recognize were still around, just much older. A lot of old people wished for roomfuls of kids and grandkids, which was funny where she thought about it.

Too tired to stay on her feet, she found a place to sit down and support the spot that was bothering her. She saw her reflection in the window, a little unnatural and decked out in a crappy outfit from six years ago.

Intuitively, Xia Bingbing found a smooth talker in the distance a little suspicious. She darted from here to there as if she knew everyone. And the strangest thing was that everyone seemed to know her. She had good looks, and her undulating voice sounded familiar.

"Isn't this Bingbing? You look exactly the same as in the pictures ... even the clothes ... are the same," she then paused abruptly. "Bingbing, do you want to meet the senior people from your dad's workplace? He isn't in Shanghai, busy like crazy. I already said hi."

"You already did, so I won't have to," Xia Bingging said in a low voice.

You said hi on his behalf, so on whose behalf should I say hi? Xia Bingbing wondered.

Without being invited, she sat down next to Xia Bingbing and said: "You know, Bingbing," she tried to hold back a smile, "I checked around and realized that you are the only one in the family without buck teeth ... Is this true? ... Talk to me ..."

A sharp look was cast her way immediately, which was when Xia Bingbing noticed the auntie and younger girl sitting across from her. This auntie wasn't the same as from when she was young. She was new and she had seen her picture in the wedding invitation. Xia Bingbing had never met the girl next to her before, and she was wearing steel braces.

She was reminded that a long long time ago, she was the same obedient sitting next to her mom at the Xia family's weddings and funerals. Her dad was busy too back then, so they were his natural deputies. After things went wrong between her dad and her mom, for a long while she was the only one attending. Now that she was sitting with someone else, no one seemed to mind. Maybe she had attached too much importance to her own feelings. Following the eyes of the girl with the braces, Xia Bingbing looked around and did spot in the distance the original younger girl from her childhood. She didn't have neat teeth either, but Xia Bingbing figured that at least she would understand her. She just hoped that she wouldn't turn out the way she had.

# 4

Xia Bingbing was the only one of the younger generation who didn't have buck teeth, because her dad was the only one of his generation who was equally blessed. Zhou Lei had some buck teeth, although Uncle Zhou didn't, so maybe legacy from that mysterious mom of Zhou Lei's? Xia Bingbing lost herself in the speculation, so that when she reported back to her mom on the funeral, her mom gave her a good tongue-lashing.

"What are you good for if you can't remember anything. I have raised you for nothing!" "Did he already get a certificate with this woman?"

"Not sure. She is supposed to be the girlfriend."

"Where are they getting married? At your dad's old place? Or do they plan to buy a new place?"

"Not sure. I heard that they are waiting to be relocated by the government."

"Relocation? That woman knows what she is doing. Looks like she has it in for your dad. What else did she say to you?"

"Nothing much. She just sat real close to me and held my hands."

"She really doesn't mind putting on a show. Let me tell you, Bingbing, you need to find out about it from your dad. Your name is still registered with that old place, you know? If you don't agree, they can't move anywhere. Go as soon as you can. When is he coming back?"

"Mom, I have a tummy ache."

"And I have a headache. Look at you, what can you do? You taught kindergarten and had parents complain about you. You worked the front desk and lost your boss's stuff. The only thing you are good for is living off us. But I still have to find you a job one way or another. You can't stay like this, too embarrassing for me."

"Bingbing, listen to me, if your dad talks about the old place with you, you ask for three hundred thousand yuan, not a penny less, do you understand? Get lost if you can't get that amount from him. That place was assigned by my dad's workplace when I married your dad, it's mine, don't you ever forget."

"Got it, three hundred thousand."

Uncle Zhou came back with a bag of small peanuts. Pea-sized sweat rolled down the creases on his face to his neck.

"Do you know that weather forecast for today is forty degrees, never this high before. Are you hot?"

Her mom wiped the sweat off her nose with an exaggerated gesture. "Of course. What did you buy again? It's all food with you!" She stood up and dug out some peanuts from the plastic bag in Uncle Zhou's hand and peeled away.

"Zhou Lei came by today," Uncle Zhou directed the words at her mom while glancing Xia Bingbing's way.

"What does he want?" her mom asked.

"Just to see me. So you only allow your daughter to be close to you and not my son to be close to me? Come on."

"Don't lie to me. I know you. Did he give you money? Was that why you bought stuff? Hand me the money." Her mom gave him the usual evil eye and said to Xia Bingbing, "Set the table, let's eat."

Xia Bingbing stood up with difficulty and made her way to the kitchen. She felt nauseous from time to time, especially at seeing the dishes on the table with the vegetables indistinguishable from the meat. Her face felt intolerably greasy and the pores on her arms were swollen and causing her pain. She strained to pick up the thermal bottle and poured water into the wash basin.

"Zhou Lei said he is going to Dongguan ..." Uncle Zhou said.

"To do what? Work as a day laborer? He isn't thinking straight."

"He said hi to you and Bingbing."

"Oh, that's nice of him. I was the one who helped him with everything, like enlisting in the army and whatnot. So what if his mom is a foreigner? She does nothing for him. If he knows what he is doing, he should treat us nice in the future ..."

Xia Bingbing subconsciously turned down the cold water. She pulled down the towel, gently squeezed out the water and leaned against the sink.

Bingbing? ... Bingbing?

Xia Bingbing jerked her head around to see her mom standing behind her with a cold look.

"Go change your pants, you got it on the pants."

"Oh," Bingbing answered, still in a half-daze.

Her mom and Uncle Zhou quite enjoyed that meal. The harmony between them painted a depressing picture of happiness for Xia Bingbing. But she couldn't shake off the feeling that it's not completely inconceivable that these two seemingly lovey dovey people would one day turn against each other over money or some other thing.

Uncle Zhou found another job for Xia Bingbing, to keep an eye on a store and to start in fall. He did take care of her and did behave himself towards her, if she was honest with herself. Xia Bingbing knew that he would stoop down for a lot of things, but he wasn't the worst seed. They could never become father and daughter, or friends from different generations. They got on each other's nerves more than strangers, but weren't sworn enemies either. Xia Bingbing couldn't tell what they had between them.

Xia Bingbing heard the clock at midnight and her heart started itching out of habit. She could no longer avoid such waiting and torture anymore. Amid the turning of the ceiling fan and the rubbing of bodies on the bamboo bedding, she heard one hand sliding onto the other person with greed and the other person pretending to fend it off, silent foreplay accompanied by some fragrant spray. Cicadas were crying themselves hoarse outside the window. They couldn't see her, but she could stare at the small squares on the screen window, eyes wide open, and watch little insects that she couldn't name trying to find their way in. She only allowed herself shallow breaths, because the slightest movement from her would stop those above her. Sometimes she didn't want them to stop, even though she was disgusted every time she visualized their faces.

She had to face such nights alone now that Zhou Lei was gone. She remembered that the first time Zhou Lei and she stared at each other was at night, too. From his sunken sofa, he gingerly turned his head, and the part of the hair that was thus released looked ugly the way it should. He looked at her sleeping on the floor, and it was the first time she saw such an understanding look, so she was surprised and warmed. Xia Bingbing didn't think there would ever be another person on this earth who could give her such a bright and empathetic look. This kind of feeling came only once in a lifetime, so the first time was also the only time. He would never look at her the same way as he did the first time. Even though she was only thirteen then and Zhou Lei was fifteen.

She had believed that Zhou Lei would be the only one in the family to treat her nice. He promised as much. But he still left first. Maybe he had been right.

If only I could have died that day, Xia Bingbing often thought. The more she thought about it, the harder she pushed down. Her lower tummy still hurt on and off. She had an indescribable sensation of collapsing, as if something that was originally part of her body was striving to betray her by detaching itself.

# 5

Xia Bingbing struggled out of bed after picking up a call from her dad. Even the morning was suffocating. She carried the phone and limped into the kitchen. As usual, she soaked the metal scrub, boiled water, washed her face and made tea. Covering herself with the wet and warm towel, Xia Bingbing felt herself melting and felt raw as if burned by the scorching steam.

At least mornings belonged to her, and she could do anything in front of them. They were totally oblivious and emotionless towards her, and didn't care what happened to her. Not her mom, and not the man she had to put up with.

When she was ready to go out for breakfast, her mom dragged herself out of bed to use the bathroom. She saw something and yelled: "Look, look at you, so filthy, take a look yourself, all over the floor ..."

Xia Bingbing pulled up her pants, then immediately

squatted down to wipe along the floor.

"You are using the mop for the table. What were you thinking this early in the morning, you are in your twenties, so embarrassing ..."

Xia Bingbing looked up with a smile and said: "Mom, Dad has agreed to three hundred thousand."

Her mom took a long pause before tucking in her hair and turning around for the bathroom. "Should have asked for more," the words trailed behind her.

Xia Bingbing used all her strength to rinse the mop. The bloody water splashed onto her arms before sliding down of its own volition.

# 6

Her dad was getting married. Xia Bingbing saw two new pillows at his place, and a new comforter. She had the sudden urge to sleep next to their bed. The floor next to their bed would have sufficed, as long as it's not a smell she was familiar with or a spot she was familiar with.

Xia Bingbing had arranged to meet her dad in the bank and he asked her to go to his place first. On her way in, she saw him already dressed up and putting on his shoes with a shoehorn that didn't quite work. Xia Bingbing had the urge to cry. She recalled that a long long time ago, when she was still wearing that outfit from when she was young, she went to her dad's place for money. Before she left, he asked her whether she had money for the bus. She shook her head and he started looking for money in his wallet, his back pockets and the inside pockets of his clothes. Yellowish fifty yuan notes were lying right next to his cigarettes, but he was determined to find a ten yuan note for her, breaking out in sweat with the effort.

She had the same urge to cry back then, because she simply couldn't tell whether the person in front of her loved her.

Her dad said over the phone that this was the last time he

was giving her money, and the money this time included money for her wedding, because he was getting married himself and would have less to spare.

Xia Bingbing said: "Fine."

Her dad asked: "Your mom put you up to it, right?"

Xia Bingbing said: "Right."

Her dad said: "I know you wouldn't be the one asking."

Xia Bingbing said: "… Actually I need it."

Her dad said: "Ok then, come over to my place when you have time."

Xia Bingbing didn't think they would have said any of those things to each other had they been face to face. But she was just speculating.

She saw her dad walking towards her, expressionless, before suddenly holding her up.

"Bingbing? Bingbing? Are you ok? Why do you have blood on you …"

"Sure … sure, let's hurry to the bank, then you can go home and rest."

# 7

The day Bingbing regained consciousness, there was a thunderstorm in Dongguan and one person died. She heard the news from the radio her mom brought to her hospital bed and got a little worried.

Her mom felt lucky that she didn't collapse until she had got home from the money transfer. She couldn't have lived down such an embarrassment. But later on, she figured it was no big deal, since the times were different. Her only wish now was to marry Bingbing off as soon as possible after her hospitalization. Uncle Zhou suggested looking for someone from the countryside who had land and house. People in the city were crammed together and getting poorer in the crammed condition. Besides, the way she was now, she couldn't really hope for better.

As for the metal scrub taken out of Xia Bingbing's lower body, Uncle Zhou said to her mom when no one was listening: "Maybe she wanted it too much." Xia Bingbing overheard it later, as they talked about it several times again. But she knew that Uncle Zhou wasn't really the worst kind.

# I Really Don't Want to Come

The door squeaked open when Luo Qingqing pushed it. The lock was long gone and beyond repair since the ground was sinking. Mom was coming out with a dustpan and glanced at her: "Why did you come so late? Go on in to kowtow."

Mom passed her through the narrow doorway and brushed against her shoulder, not exactly in a light way. Luo Qingqing looked down at the black piling in the dustpan which seemed to be wriggling and grossed her out. A dusty smoke enveloped the room and invisible particles were fighting over each other to invade every single organ in her. She figured her eyes were playing tricks on her, or ... maybe there was nothing wriggling. What really grossed her out was the room itself, with a force that attached itself to her with an intimacy she hadn't been able to shake off or flee all these years.

A round tabletop had been placed on the dining table, taking over the entire room unapologetically. Stools with peeling paint circled the table. The room wasn't normally so crowded, but became artificially so when a dozen or so seats had to be set up for dinner. The mirror was covered by cloth and the lights were off as usual. Unsteady candlelight from the round tabletop had a dizzying effect. Seeing how Grandma was on her knees chanting towards the candlelight, eyes closed, Luo Qingqing sat down quietly on the sofa to the side.

This tableau inside the room couldn't have been more familiar, and the setup had been the same since Luo Qingqing's earliest memory. At every such worshipping ritual in her childhood, Grandma would admonish her and her cousin repeatedly not to run around or to bump into any chair, even though no one was sitting on any chair.

Luo Qingqing sat on the sofa, staring into space. She was thinking that it was a long time ago that this room had felt really alive. She, Dad, Mom, Auntie, Uncle and her cousin, they would sit around on New Year's Eve, while Grandma was busy cooking and Grandpa was busy pouring the drink. A plate overflowing with hairy crabs occupied the center of the table, and steam from hot dishes on the table rose slowly up to the bleached ceiling and took its sweet time seeping into it. Chicken, ducks and eels were hung up in the courtyard, and seafood had to be placed in the bathtub. There was still surplus food at the end of the holiday, because people would bring Grandpa tons of holiday food while he was still working. The fun-loving Grandpa was now reduced to watching the decline and chaos of the room with cool objectiveness. Luo Qingqing had only vague impressions of Grandpa whose bloodless face in his funeral picture looked strange to her. She couldn't even reconstruct scenes of living with Grandpa. But for whatever reason, she had started missing him more over the years. He was the soul of the family and even though silent now, he was still an unshakable force that permeated the air inside the room.

No one could capture it, and no one could erase it.

No change and exactly the same as more than a decade ago. Still two comforters on the bed, and Grandma would spread out the other comforter every night before bed and fold it up again in the morning. She never tired of it and even kept three pillows on Grandpa's side for him to lean on because of his heart condition ... because she was the only one in the family with the firm belief that Grandpa would come back.

What else hadn't changed? Eating at home on New Year's Eve had become less popular now. But since there were only three left in the family, plus spiritual presences around the table for show, it was no fun wherever the dinner was. Grandma still went about the unreal setup with the same gusto, year after year. Because she was the only one in the family who believed that at least everything should look the same as before.

Two mats were placed on the floor, one facing the candlelight on the round tabletop and the other facing the low square table. The Earth Deity and another deity, name unknown, sat on the low square table facing the south and the north, respectively. White bowls held warmed alcohol, surrounded by several steamy vegetable dishes. There were many more dishes on the round tabletop, beckoning with their white steam. But hot dishes weren't meant for consumption. After Grandpa passed away, Grandma lost herself in ancestor and deity worshipping. So Luo Qingqing never got to eat any freshly cooked hot dish on New Year's Eve ever since.

Luo Qingqing had slept poorly last night and protested to Mom that she had had enough of the worshipping. But Mom said: "Grandma doesn't have much to live for, and you will deprive her of even that?"

Grandma finally opened her squinting eyes and looked at Luo Qingqing kindly, which made Luo Qingqing suddenly regret her insistence of last night.

"You are here, Qingqing. Come and kowtow to the ancestors." Grandma rose with difficulty and gave up her mat.

The flickering candlelight hurt Luo Qingqing's eyes, and what Grandma said gently trampled over her rationalization. Her heart twisted into painful knots as she looked at Grandma's face, the pain outweighing the grievance when she swore last night that she would never kneel again. Grandma was already in her seventies, so she was being willful instead of Grandma being stubborn. How could Grandma have known how reluctant she was. Grandma's giving her mat to her had strangled, like a ruthless rope, her passionate expectations for the New Year.

This mat was so familiar, having stuck around for eighteen years. Grandma's needlework on it had lasted through the years, despite the lint balls all over it. Ever since she could remember, she had been kneeling towards this direction asking to be blessed by invisible ancestors. Every New Year's Eve for eighteen years, she would walk the same distance to come here, stepping over crimson shreds of lit fireworks and listening to family reunion behind every front door. Nothing had shifted and nothing had changed, the good being still good and the evil being still evil. Luo Qingqing was agitated by this endless cycle, but she was powerless to change anything, so she had to put aside all her principles for reasons of "I really can't" or "I really shouldn't".

She felt humiliated, but could do nothing about it. The candlelight played over Grandma's weathered face, a little showy and a little charming, losing itself on the trembling lips chanting ghostly notes. Luo Qingqing knew that Grandma would never notice her reluctance and that Grandma still liked her no matter what. It was the mindless still objects and unpredictable air in the room that were emanating ferocity, so how could she take it out on an elderly person?

Besides, Grandma has always been fair, like when she and her cousin were splitting cookies and no one was allowed to take more than the other. Actually Grandma and she had been growing closer over the years, even though Grandma would still never verbally abuse her. Her cousin wasn't so lucky. Grandma was always nagging at him and belittling him, which hadn't damaged their feelings towards each other. Luo Qingqing understood in her heart that Grandma let her have her ways. As for the worshipping, Grandma didn't know and wouldn't have forced her had she known.

No one was forcing her, which was exactly why she didn't

know whom to say no to.

At the same moment Mom stepped in, Luo Qingqing knelt down peacefully. She sighed gently, although everything around her had grown oblivious to her grievance.

Facing the two empty stools, she kowtowed three times, quietly.

"Your mom already kowtowed. Why don't you get some rest in the small room, and come out and talk to Grandpa once the incense is half way down."

"Sure," Mom answered briskly for Luo Qingqing. Luo Qingqing stood up listlessly and saw Mom easily maneuver her way through that circle of empty stools to put the dustpan back in the courtyard. Luo Qingqing figured that Mom should have worshipped many more times than she did, but things never looked up for her and how could she not despair? Luo Qingqing was puzzled and felt bad for Mom. She witnessed Grandma growing more hunchbacked year after year, and Mom stopping crying when no one was watching and grinding her teeth through it all, just as they witnessed her unstoppable growing. But how could eyes do more to convey the caring they had for each other? All they were capable of were superficial condolences for the other generation's sorrow.

More than a dozen identical glasses and bowls were laid out on the round tabletop, and Grandma might be the only one who could tell which ones belonged to Grandpa. Grandpa used to take Grandma on a trip around New Year every year, until the first year after his retirement when no one offered the elderly couple any joy ride anymore. Luo Qingqing vaguely recalled that Grandpa spent the whole morning that day calling around for a car and somberly closed his address book in the end. He remained expressionless and looked even slow when Grandma put in front of him his drink for that meal. On a normal day he would have pestered Grandma for more, like a kid begging for candies.

Luo Qingqing was still in primary school that year and had forgotten everything else. She did remember clearly that Grandpa didn't drink that half glass that day.

Because soon afterwards Grandpa had a heart attack and was hospitalized, which was soon followed by Luo Qingqing's tenth birthday. A birthday meal was exchanged for porridge. Looking at Grandpa's purplish face, Luo Qingqing felt selfish displeasure. She could never forget that displeasure. Her first major birthday had gone down the drain just like that, and if it had been one day earlier or one day later, she wouldn't have been so disappointed. Luo Qingqing didn't realize till Dad deserted the family later that her aborted tenth birthday celebration was just the beginning of a series of natural deaths. The entire family would never have the chance to eat at the same table again, and happiness and hardship would never walk hand in hand again. Not for her twentieth birthday, not for her thirtieth birthday … maybe never.

Luo Qingqing sat silently on the tinfoil-covered recliner, her rootless upbringing and slightly indifferent heartache playing back in her mind like a movie. But even her memory was an intricate incompletion, and where she found herself at that moment couldn't have been closer to images remembered. Numbing time was the only moving element and everything else had been preserved in perfection. And the perfection itself was causing the panic. But reality could never withstand as close a look as memory, just as memory was never as cruel as reality.

"Your grandma can't keep things neat, take a look, people would have said she had been abandoned had they seen … I just finished shoving out the anthill, so gross. Your grandma won't hurt anything live and keeps even ants around," Mom complained to Luo Qingqing when she walked in with grapes she had just washed.

Hair rose at the back of Luo Qingqing's neck when she realized that what she saw in the dustpan at the doorway was really a wriggling life form.

But as she recalled, Grandpa and Mom were very much alike, tolerant, hard-working and neat-freak. With Grandma, Mom would butt heads sometimes, but that was a long time ago. Now Mom compromised on everything with Grandma, which was what Grandpa did when he was alive. After he passed way, Grandma became more and more pathetic.

Grandma had ambitions and knew what she was doing. Before she was even twenty, she left her hometown to work in Shanghai alone and sent money back home for her younger siblings to go to school. Giving birth to Mom and Auntie took a toll on her health, so she had no more children. According to Mom, Grandpa had a vasectomy in his thirties which came even to the attention of senior people at his workplace. But it was because Grandma's firm "No" had stumped all kind-hearted intervention and Grandpa's wish for a son.

Thinking about all these, Luo Qingqing admired Grandma, but she also felt sentimental. The past was so distant from her, and all she could see now was Grandma's permanently chanting lips and her stumbling around to set up such a hollow show.

Things would never be the same again, maybe that's what it meant.

Like Grandpa spoiled Mom most. One time Mom reported cryingly that she had accidentally touched a toad. Grandpa pulled every string and even personally contacted the team leader of Mom's farm work unit. A few days later Mom was transferred from the farm to the village-affiliated factory and never set foot again in the mud on the farmland even when an extra pair of hands could have been used. Losing Grandpa spelt the end of all happiness for Mom, but of course Mom had never put it in so many words. Luo Qingqing just lamented at the helplessness when faced with the vicissitudes of life. Sometimes losing a person led to the loss of a whole chunk of good life, both in the present and in the future. He had been so important, like a small umbrella trying to shield as much as it could and being blamed for not being big enough when occasionally things didn't turn out the expected way. Then the umbrella broke and the rain came down soaking. When life came at you guns ablaze, you realized that someone had carried you and taken the bullet for you.

"I don't want any," Luo Qingqing pushed away the grapes in Mom's hand. "Auntie's family bailed out again?" she asked pointedly.

"Don't mention this to Grandma, you need to be understanding, you know. It's New Year, so don't ruin it." Mom peeled a grape and stuffed it in Luo Qingqing's mouth. Luo Qingqing had to swallow her retort and spit out the grape seeds, twitching her lips.

Mom started digging at the tinfoil dust in the table crevices, scattering silver dust that ended up in every corner of the furniture where it would stay forever by the look of it.

Luo Qingqing almost jumped at the sharp snap of a fingernail breaking.

"Qingqing, it's time!" Grandma called from the next room.

"You could have answered. What are you thinking all the time?" Mom pulled gently at the still attached fingernail, folded a corner of the mop and continued to dig at the table crevices.

Grandma had moved over the red bricks and iron basin for the ritual. The red candles on the round tabletop were already half way gone, and melted candle had piled up on the table shamelessly. Luo Qingqing thought about Mom's newly broken fingernail and wondered how Mom was going to get the dirty piling off later.

Luo Qingqing went up to the mat again, not knowing what to think. She didn't hesitate this time and just wanted to get the annoying ritual over with. She knelt down emotionlessly and was ready to kowtow.

"Qingqing, whatever wish you have, you can tell Grandpa. With his blessing, your wishes will come true." Grandma spoke again in her kind voice which reverberated gently on Luo

Qingqing's eardrums.

I wish ... that there will be no more worshipping next year.

Luo Qingqing murmured in her heart while feeling guilty.

She prayed piously, but never believed that her wishes could be granted that way. Growing up hadn't been without struggle, but with her own feeble efforts and Mom's around-the-clock care, she was finally eighteen this year.

She had a million things on her mind, but had to force herself to be calm.

No point not being calm.

One ... two ... three.

Luo Qingqing was about to stand up.

"Qingqing, some more kowtowing for your dad and cousin," Grandma instructed slowly, praying beads twisted around her hands and face deeply lined.

With one look at Grandma's weathered face, Luo Qingqing turned her head and adjusted her position so as to face the obscure candlelight, the dirty melted candle, the tableful of invisible deceased and the dishes that had lost all steam ...

One ... two ... three ...

One ... two... three ...

"Grandma, why is Junjun not coming?" Luo Qingqing stood up and asked in a deliberately loud voice without looking at Mom.

Next to her, Mom gave her the evil eye.

Grandma said, reassured: "Tomorrow, he will definitely come tomorrow." Then she rose to fetch the folded paper bullions and stumbled before Luo Qingqing caught her in time.

Grandma spent all year folding paper bullions and would have several bagfuls for every New Year's worshipping. Buddhism preached leaving everything behind, so how could she be allowed to bring such bulky possessions with her to the other side? But then, who would deny someone already in her seventies?

After her own kowtowing, Mom got up and tried to give Grandma a hand, but Grandma insisted on walking on her own, and she didn't look at all weakened as she turned down Mom's offer. She had put up a brave front for several decades, but still ended up so desolate. Mom was so right, Grandma was pathetic.

Luo Qingqing's emotions vacillated between resistance and resignation every single moment, and she was more and more convinced that home wasn't the place for reasoning. Sometimes she held it in, but other times she just had to vent the unfairness she felt. She was the school's number one recommendation for exemption from college entrance exams, and the school had taught her to help build the country through freedom, harmony and science education. Yet none of these stood a chance against Grandma's gentle command to kowtow, and it had been like this for eighteen years … She wanted to know when she could have a New Year that would truly belong to her.

One year's worth of Grandma's efforts and blessings was burning away in the basin. Luo Qingqing helped to throw the paper bullions in and was choked to tears. She recalled that she and her cousin would fight over who got to throw the bullions and Auntie would rush over to take her cousin away from being burned. She had laughed at her cousin for chickening out, but in retrospect, how could Auntie have left her alone beside the basin …

"I always wish all of you well, and I keep asking Buddha," Grandma started praying.

"I have a daughter Shanshan, and I wish her health and early retirement."

"I have a son-in-law Luo Kang …"

"He isn't anymore!" Mom cut in. "Why are you still …"

"I wish that he treats Qingqing well and enjoys his work," Grandma went on, totally deaf to Mom's same-worded protest over the past several years.

"I have a granddaughter Qingqing, and I wish that she gets smarter and gets into college."

"Did you hear that, Qingqing? Grandma has always prayed for you, that's why you got into the foreign language university." Luo Qingqing kept burning the bullions and ignored Mom.

"I have a younger daughter Pingping, poor thing, and I wish that she gets well soon. My son-in-law Baochang, I wish that his business grows bigger. And I have a grandson Junjun, I wish that he goes all the way to become a Ph.D."

Luo Qingqing was taken by surprise and she didn't know why. For years, the wording hadn't changed, except for the last sentence which was completely new and breathtaking. Her cousin wasn't here, so she wondered whose ears it was intended for, hopefully Buddha's. She had never been the preferred one growing up, so this vying for attention wasn't really her thing.

With a small sigh, Luo Qingqing threw in more bullions and saw them gradually turning from silver to red and from red to black. They wilted and curled up, and in those few short seconds it took for them to disintegrate into apathetic ashes, the expectations, longings, memories and tangible wealth in this world had been transferred to the netherworld. It's true whether one chose to believe it or not. That's the way with everything, no logic to it.

"Oh, what was it that fell in?" Grandma stuck her head above the basin to look and Mom grabbed her leaning body.

The flame shot up with a boom and Luo Qingqing fell back on the mat. The room was enveloped in thick smoke and it took a while for Luo Qingqing to see clearly the scared faces of Mom and Grandma and their ash-covered hair.

"Mom, what did you throw in there? See how dangerous it is, don't burn the bullions on your own from now on! You have to have us with you when you do it!" Mom led Grandma to sit on the bed, and Grandma looked all shaken and kept blessing herself under her breath. Luo Qingqing caressed Grandma's hunched back and told her again and again that it was all right.

Pale ashes were everywhere in the room and floating down proudly onto the TV, the bed and even the stools where ancestors were supposed to be sitting. Some of the ashes brushed against the indifferent red candlelight before ingratiating themselves with the melted candle. The rearing incense sticks were almost burned out, and the slightest touch by the floating ashes toppled the long buildup of incense ashes.

They didn't feel the pain ... which was good, Luo Qingqing thought and got a little jealous for no apparent reason.

Luo Qingqing looked into the basin and felt the still intense hot air. A charred lighter lay peacefully inside and had already turned black. Its sacrifice hadn't succeeded in bringing everything down, which was a pity. This New Year was gaining in solemnity, and maybe they had escaped unharmed thanks to the blessings from the tableful of deities. No matter what, Luo Qingqing realized that Grandma was getting too old for worshipping, which she insisted on, without their help. Disaster could strike any minute otherwise. No longer was it about whether to put up with it, or about who was right and who was wrong.

What was it about then? Luo Qingqing couldn't quite vocalize it, but at least next year and the year after that, she would have to continue kowtowing. No matter whether she was a college student or not, eighteen or twenty, whether she majored in English or some other thing, whether she was accomplished or came to nothing, as soon as she set foot inside this door in disrepair, as soon as she saw those people who were closest to her, she was nothing, or rather, she was nothing but daughter ...

Mom wrapped up the basin and took it to the courtyard. Luo Qingqing heard Mom turn on the faucet and a loud sizzling sound.

Grandma started cleaning up the bowls and chopsticks, and the dishes were ash-speckled. Luo Qingqing helped to move the stools, thinking that the ancestors were finally done with the feast and ready to leave, satisfied that the living had subjected themselves to them. There wasn't much in this world anyway, and death seemed a better choice since it was worshipped and company was provided.

It was another world outside the window. The sound of firecrackers was heard from time to time, and became suffocating when it came in quick succession. Was there really that much to cheer for, Luo Qingqing wondered as she half-heartedly got rice for everyone.

Luo Qingqing sometimes admired Mom a lot. She played daughter with abandon, with no regret and no thought of ever quitting. Luo Qingqing knew that she could never compare with Mom. Although she tried to help, she didn't feel up to it. She was opinionated and impetuous, and her face revealed everything.

Mom busied herself between the kitchen and the living room. Luo Qingqing heard the banging of utensils, opening and closing of the fridge, and the microwave being turned on. Everything was as orderly as an assembly line. Mom replaced the ash-contaminated dishes with those originally prepared for the next day. It was astounding how fast she cleaned up. By the time Luo Qingqing brought the rice, the round tabletop had already been taken down and the dishes warmed up. The green leaves of the vegetables were tinged yellowish, although no one had touched them. But Luo Qingqing had no appetite whatsoever, ashes or no ashes.

Mom kept serving her food. Luo Qingqing noticed that Mom's fingernails had turned slightly pink and thought about the hardened melted candle on the table just now.

She bent her head and chewed her rice, hurting inside.

Grandma ate little, maybe because the day had tired her out, maybe because of that scare. She had an inscrutable look on her face and an ungratified expression, as if she wasn't suffering enough or satisfied with herself enough. She had a faint but dejected smile. Tenderness and love lingered on, however, so she wasn't exactly sad.

"Qingqing," Grandma put down her chopsticks. "Tomorrow Grandma will give you and your cousin money for the New Year. You will have more than Junjun, so don't tell, got it?"

Got it.

Luo Qingqing acknowledged. Every New Year's Eve Grandma would remind her and had never forgotten once.

"Mom, how do you tell which one has more and which has less?" Mom asked smilingly.

Grandma grinned, stood up and went to the closet. She took out a key ring from her pocket and picked the right one for the closet. After taking out two identical red envelopes, she locked the closet again.

"Look carefully. This one is for Qingqing, three hundred yuan, which were laid flat," Grandma said slowly, her finger gliding over it.

"This one is for Junjun, I am folding it in half." Grandma pinched the folding line, her face unusually animated.

With that, Grandma put the red envelopes in her pocket and returned to the previous inscrutable ungratified expression. With a faint smile, she took some food. The crows' feet that had unfolded just now were squeezed back together again.

"Isn't Grandma smart?" Mom nudged at Luo Qingqing's arm. Luo Qingqing nodded her heart-felt admiration for Grandma's smarts. But joking aside, she felt uneasy, as this meal every year tended to make her uneasy for reasons she couldn't tell.

"Shanshan, I have something to discuss with you." Grandma looked at Mom and put down her chopsticks.

"What is it?"

"Before the New Year, Pingping and Baochang came by, although Baochang didn't come in. Pingping asked me for the property deeds and residence registration, saying that she needed them for the government relocation of her mother-in-law's place, to get more compensation."

"Oh." Mom grew a little glum.

Grandma looked at Mom apologetically: "The way they asked, I couldn't turn them down, but they will definitely bring them back, you can be sure of that. But I do want you to know that I don't have the property deeds with me now."

Dead silence ensued in the room, and firecrackers started up again outside the window. The entire apartment complex was like a frying pan torturing everyone with noises. They couldn't hear anything the others said, their murmuring or monologue drowned out by the gigantic sound waves ushering in the New Year. No difference could be heard between forgiveness, tolerance, apathy and pain.

"Don't you worry, Mom, we won't ask for anything. Qingqing and I will always be with you, right, Qingqing?"

Luo Qingqing nodded. She saw Grandma smile embarrassedly, but it could have been a genuine smile.

For the New Year's worshipping, Grandma had got up at four in the morning to pray and buy groceries. She insisted on a full-blown show for the New Year and managed a tableful of dishes no matter how many were coming for the New Year's Eve dinner. Luo Qingqing and Mom left soon after dinner. On the way home, Luo Qingqing held Mom's hand. Kids were running around the streets lighting fireworks and the sky was illuminated in all colors. It was so harmonious and so cheery. But Mom kept up a brisk pace all the way.

"Mom, I want to cry," Luo Qingqing said dejectedly.

"One more day tomorrow, let's get it over with, then you can go out with your schoolmates." Mom had other things on her mind, Luo Qingqing could tell.

It's true that tomorrow would be even harder to survive. She despaired at the endless cycle year after year. Whatever her progress or aspiration during the year, the year always ended like this. Or rather, the year always started like this.

"Mom, are you happy that I can go to college without taking the entrance exams? If you don't think the foreign language university is good enough, I think I can try harder for a better one." Luo Qingqing changed the subject. Holding tight to Mom's arm, she seemed to have regained strength. Maybe she hoped to give herself more confidence for the New Year. The day that she had just had was certainly a letdown.

"Of course I am happy. You are where my hope is in this life. Mom is happy for you whichever college you get into."

"Then I will try harder and maybe I can get to go to Beijing?" Luo Qingqing asked.

"Are you leaving me?" Mom suddenly looked at her in astonishment and murmured after a long pause: "What's wrong with Shanghai? What's there in Beijing?"

"How can I be leaving you?" Luo Qingqing realized that she had made a similar promise to Mom as Mom had to Grandma. She was rattled and smiled without feeling it.

When Luo Qingqing woke up the next morning, Mom had long left for Grandma's place to help out. She took her time changing into clean clothes and didn't get to Grandma's till it was almost time to eat.

She heard Auntie giggling before entering. "Qingqing came really late. We thought we were late, but you were even more so, ha ha." Auntie's pointed laughter unsettled Luo Qingqing, so she moved to Grandma's bed and leaned on a pillow.

"Happy New Year, Auntie and Junjun. I ... am not feeling too well, have a headache, so I will lie down for a bit." Done with her greetings, Luo Qingqing planned to keep mute. This was what she normally resorted to in the presence of those two. She would either fake sickness or stare into space. She couldn't say much, because what she had to say might not come out nice. Grandma would be saddened and Mom would think she was being wayward. She didn't want this to happen, since it's New Year.

Her cousin was watching TV, and from time to time Luo Qingqing would squint at the TV screen.

Mom was rinsing the floor mop in the courtyard. Luo Qingqing heard the water running, a brisk sound in the cold outside.

"Qingqing, who got you what you are wearing?" Auntie seemed to have noticed that Luo Qingqing had wandered off in her head.

"Mom." Luo Qingqing didn't look at her.

"No wonder it makes you look older."

Luo Qingqing kept quiet and continued to watch the TV. She told herself that a sharp tongue would do her no good and tolerance was the way to go.

"What did you have yesterday? What did Grandma cook for you?" Auntie seemed to have more questions coming.

"Some vegan dishes, tasted great." Luo Qingqing wasn't in a hurry with the answer.

"Junjun, we ate too much yesterday and my stomach is still a little upset. Remember not to eat too much today. We have good stuff at home that Daddy bought. If you eat too much here and can't eat more once we get home, Daddy won't be happy."

"I will eat, don't you worry." Her cousin replied impatiently.

"Look at you, all you know is eating, ha ha." "By the way, Qingqing, how much are you paying for tutoring now?"

"… I have got into the foreign language university without exams, so I don't need tutoring anymore."

"My Junjun is tutored by certified outstanding teachers who only accept advanced students. One hundred yuan for one lesson and twice a week, keeps us really busy."

Hunched over, Grandma brought over the grapes that Mom had bought. Luo Qingqing recalled that she only had one yesterday.

Auntie peeled one. "It's pretty sweet, just too small. I never buy such small ones." Her cousin next to her had several in a row and spit out the seeds loudly. It disgusted Luo Qingqing.

"Why don't you buy some and bring over from now on, we all like big ones." Luo Qingqing looked at Mom's lonely figure in the courtyard and was too indignant to hold back a retort.

"It's not exactly on my way …" Auntie was momentarily stunned, but soon found a new comeback. Luo Qingqing stood up and headed for the kitchen, trying to shut them out.

Luo Qingqing got the chopsticks and bowls to help start lunch.

She saw that Mom finally finished setting up the mop to dry, the water drops sparkling. The weather was brilliant, even though the wintry sun was objective and unsympathetic. Mom walked in and saw what she was going, so she told her to be careful not to break anything, before she hurried to get the dishes. Luo Qingqing didn't know what to say when she noticed Mom's fingers had been turned into carrots by the cold.

She stepped into the living room only to hear her cousin ask for orange juice. Grandma asked Mom whether she had bought orange juice and Mom said only cola. Grandma immediately fished out five yuan from her pocket and put on her overcoat to go out to buy the juice. Mom stopped Grandma: "I'll go. It's so cold, an old lady like you shouldn't go out." Mom stood up to go.

"Mom, let me." Luo Qingqing put on her overcoat.

"Start without me." Luo Qingqing had been dying to go out for some fresh air but hadn't expected to benefit from such a disgusting excuse.

Mom helped Luo Qingqing button up. Luo Qingqing shot a glance at her cousin and turned around to go.

"Qingqing, you look much better with the overcoat. You are too skinny, and you don't even have to wear bras, since no one can tell, is that right Junjun?"

Taken aback, Luo Qingqing turned to look at Mom in astonishment. Mom was speechless for the moment, too.

Her cousin was lost in digging into the fresh fish.

Grandma didn't seem to have heard anything and sipped at her rice wine.

Luo Qingqing figured that it was retaliation for her earlier retort, and kept her silence in the end. She felt words surging through her brain and emotions churning around, but she couldn't utter a single word.

"Hurry back," Mom said in a low voice while caressing her fragile back.

She pushed hard on the door that was already beyond repair. A blast of cold air caught her off guard, and she choked and felt her heart freezing over.

A cleaning crew was sweeping up the colorful debris from the fireworks on the street, and kids in new clothes and new shoes were cheering over firecrackers. Luo Qingqing couldn't understand why things had gone so wrong so soon after she got there, or why she couldn't cry. She found it funny that with everything that was going on outside, she couldn't hear a single peep of her venting from the bottom of her heart. She felt that she was drowning in the New Year's powerful sounds, a drowning that was more humiliating than words alone, since having no hope for relief was even less bearable for her than being wronged.

She had lost Dad, just like Mom had lost Grandpa, but with some difference. Things hadn't been much better when Dad was still around. As a matter of fact, Dad wasn't the least like Grandpa. For this, she envied Mom. Mom was most blessed to have been shielded by Grandpa for the first half of her life. Luo Qingqing never liked people complimenting her on her independence and strong will, as she didn't see them as virtues but as the result of her having no one willing to shield her. During the silent and astounded confrontation just now, Mom hadn't spoken up for her, neither had Grandma.

So was it about her forbearance and strength, or about her

having no one to fight her battle?

Luo Qingqing arrived at a convenience store nearby. "An orange juice, please."

"Five yuan and eighty cents," the woman in the store said.

"Why is the price up, shouldn't it be five yuan?"

"Eighty is a good number for the New Year," the woman giggled just like Auntie.

"I only have five." Luo Qingqing fixed her with a freezing stare.

"How about this, you give me eighty cents next time you come, we are all from the same neighborhood ..."

"I only have five!" Luo Qingqing yelled, drowning out all other sounds. The woman was startled into dropping the orange juice.

After a long while, the woman grunted: "Come on, it's New Year, are you crazy?"

Luo Qingqing picked up the orange juice, turned around and left. She was ashamed and outraged, outraged at the shame and ashamed at the outrage.

Luo Qingqing struggled all the way about whether to go back and whether to face what had to be faced. Had she done the right thing just now by choosing not to fight back? What other verbal weapon did she have? And what other defense against such a naked attack? She dwelled on it till she reached the door with the broken lock again. She felt like a satiated ghost who had to turn back after missing the bus to the netherworld and who had become an abandoned spirit in the true sense of the word.

She hesitated for a bit before gathering up enough courage to push open the door with all her strength.

She saw Mom ladling soup into her bowl.

"Come on in, Qingqing, must be freezing outside. Mom has your soup here, come and drink it." Luo Qingqing sat down without a word. Her cousin next to her was drinking the soup, too. Luo Qingqing saw the half-demolished fish on the table and felt nauseous, so she just picked at some vegetables.

"Grandma, why are the bamboo shoots so tough?" Her cousin spit out several chewed bamboo shoots and complained to Grandma.

"Your mom brought them yesterday. I couldn't get new ones today and had to use these. Next time I will buy you tender ones." Grandma said apologetically. She couldn't drink salty pork soup herself, so she just sipped at the homemade rice wine.

Luo Qingqing couldn't tell why she hated Auntie's family so much. She had never even hated Dad for breaking up with Mom. She would often criticize herself for not being tolerant enough, but then the next meeting with Auntie and her lot would drive her to the edge again.

What's behind it all? She wasn't quite sure. Maybe she still couldn't forget the past, the things that were said, the looks that were given, and the apathy from those who, ironically enough, were related to her. Every New Year she would have a lot of flashbacks, and scenes from when she was growing up would play and replay in her head, like the New Year's Gala on TV the essence of which remained the same year after year. The passing time was the only element that had ever changed.

She recalled that when she was really young, Dad couldn't stand Auntie's family either and would fight with Mom over it. She figured that Dad must have hated Auntie's meanness and Grandma's preference for her. Dad, however, had extracted himself from it all many years before, and she had picked up where he had left off and fought with Mom who wasn't as sensitive to the unbearable. And she always ended up compromising against her will. But she couldn't just storm off, like Dad did.

She could never do that.

Luo Qingqing stood up and took the dirty dishes to the kitchen to wash. She had no desire to sit with them, not even for one extra second. Not because she had been badly treated, but because … she just didn't want to.

She turned on the faucet, squeezed out some detergent and slowly set to work scrubbing the greasy dishes.

"Junjun, see, your cousin is already helping out with washing the dishes." Hearing Grandma, Luo Qingqing subconsciously turned down the water.

"I don't need to, the maid at home will wash them."

"Ha ha," Auntie's laughter again took over the room. Trying to suppress her anger, Luo Qingqing turned the faucet to the max and allowed the freezing water to wash over her pale fingers.

Luo Qingqing dried her hands and returned to the room to sit next to Mom. Mom was almost done eating, too, and was chitchatting with the rest of them.

"Sister, what's in that box in your bag?" Auntie pointed at Mom's bag to the side.

"Oh, this girl here bought them for me, facial masks just for fun. I have no time, so I left them here with Mom. It was before the New Year and she could have found better use for the money." Smiling, Mom pretended to admonish Luo Qingqing.

"Junjun, Qingqing was awarded money at the English competition and bought Grandma a jade pendant. Will you do the same?" Grandma looked at her cousin expectantly.

Her cousin nodded: "I will buy Grandma a house in the future."

Grandma broke into a wide smile, took two red envelopes from her pocket, and gave one to Luo Qingqing and the other to her cousin. Luo Qingqing saw Grandma's fingers gliding over the envelopes to double check the difference. She didn't have the heart to take it at that moment. It was money given by Mom and Grandma had saved every penny.

"Grandma, didn't we agree when I was young that I would stop taking New Year's money at eighteen?" Luo Qingqing handed the money back.

Grandma was adamant: "Your award money didn't count. And you have no job. You are still a child."

Mom signaled to Luo Qingqing not to take the money, so she handed it back again.

"Mom, she already said you don't have to give money since she is making money, so why are you insisting?" Strangely enough, Auntie was taking their side which didn't happen often. Luo Qingqing frowned and kept quiet.

Grandma ended up leaving the money with Mom. After cleaning up, Mom helped Grandma massage her back in another room. Grandma's back was acting up again, maybe from the overexertion. Mom was looking everywhere for her rubbing oil and Grandma was leaning to the side, holding her cousin's hand and grinning. Luo Qingqing paced around. She didn't want to go into the room where Auntie was. She would have liked to go home, but realized it wasn't time yet.

"Qingqing," Auntie called her, but was hardly audible.

"Yes?"

"Come over here for a second." Auntie pulled her next to her, to a position where Grandma and Mom were blocked from view. Luo Qingqing kept her eyes down. She didn't want to face her, maybe because she was afraid that she would burst into abject tears over how she had been treated just now. She was worried that she still wanted something from this woman.

"Qingqing, Auntie's begging you, can you drop by my place this New Year? I will pay for your taxi."

Luo Qingqing tried to hide her surprise. She hadn't expected this from Auntie. But she didn't agree, because she would never again set foot in that place that had once freaked her out.

"Can you say yes? Auntie will give you money." With that, Auntie really took several reddish notes from her pocket and stuffed them into Luo Qingqing's hand. Luo Qingqing had thought rich people's money would be all crispy, but it turned out to be the same wrinkled.

"I don't need money." Luo Qingqing pushed it away, just like she did with the New Year's money from Grandma. She lifted her head and was surprised to see Auntie in tears.

"What's going on? Auntie, don't do this, it's New Year. You were fine just now. I don't want your money, and you are not ... exactly loaded." Luo Qingqing hesitated before speaking the truth. Auntie had been on sick leave for many years, and was supported by her husband who had his own business.

"You know your uncle has been asking for several years, how come my side of the family never visits ... No matter what, drop by this year. Please say yes?" Auntie's tears looked as unreal as if they had been painted on her face. Luo Qingqing was astonished to find herself softening her stance.

Hadn't he married the ailing Auntie so as to be able to register his residence? And hadn't he bid his time and eventually struck rich?

Hadn't he called Grandpa "Dad Dad Dad" but never popped in an appearance after Grandpa passed away?

So what did he mean saying that her side of the family "never visits"?

Luo Qingqing was very puzzled.

Mom came out of the other room at that moment:

"What are you doing here? Mom already turned in."

Auntie took one last look at Luo Qingqing and turned around for the other room, the three hundred yuan already in Luo Qingqing's grip. She had no intention of telling Mom, because she didn't think Auntie would want Mom to know.

But to go or not to go, she couldn't make up her mind. She couldn't forget the past, but couldn't resist such pleading.

Auntie was of the older generation, after all.

Luo Qingqing told Mom that she would go home first to rest. Before leaving, Luo Qingqing glanced at Auntie. She caught Auntie pulling out a facial mask that she had given Mom and stealthily stuffing it into her pants pocket. She seemed to have returned to her usual self, self-centered and a little nutty, and totally unworthy of sympathy.

On the bus home, the heat was on very high and Luo Qingqing loosened her scarf. She was dazzled by the shop windows with New Year sale signs, and by the cheery crowd milling around. She had a sudden flashback to another New Year a long time ago. She went with her cousin to his place to download on the PC the form for an English competition. Her parents had just divorced and she had no PC at home. Before they left for his place, her cousin said he had change, so Luo Qingqing didn't ask for bus fare from Mom. They ended up at the bus station witnessing one bus drive by after another. Her cousin's indifference puzzled Luo Qingqing before the puzzlement turned into sadness, which then turned into objectiveness. It was in the depth of winter and Luo Qingqing remembered her tying her scarf tighter subconsciously.

After more than one hour, a regular bus finally arrived. There was no heat on the bus, so the fare was one yuan less.

Luo Qingqing had always regretted not getting bus fare from Mom that day. She would never forget the waiting, nor the sense of shame in the ruthless cold. She even had the recurring dream that one bus after another and one crowd after another just ran their eyes all over her. She even dreamt that with nothing on, she stood in the bone-chilling wind into the night and then into dawn. While she was lost in these unhappy thoughts, the bus ambled past the Rundong supermarket across from Grandma's place. Luo Qingqing took a close look and saw two familiar figures … So those two left early too. Luo Qingqing looked on as Auntie and her cousin carried the food Grandma had given them onto the supermarket's free shuttle that would take them to the most populated apartment community in this area.

Luo Qingqing sighed gently. She recalled Auntie admonishing her cousin not to eat too much, and recalled that all rumpled up and stuffed in that woman's pocket was a facial mask she had bought Mom. She was overwhelmed by indescribable emotions, and she felt that everything was weird and suffocating.

On the second day of the New Year, Grandma came to eat at Luo Qingqing's place. Mom got up early to prepare a tableful of vegan dishes. Grandma brought many fruits, saying that she knew Mom didn't like to spend on fruits, so she had bought them especially for Luo Qingqing. While Mom was busying herself, Luo Qingqing smiled at Grandma respectfully, but the two of them had nothing to talk about. It was an awkward moment. Grandma's fruits were placed on the window sill and the jade pendant Luo Qingqing had bought her was around her neck. Luo Qingqing was warmed at the sight, but couldn't find adequate words to express it. She struggled in her head and ended up prolonging her silence, which she blamed herself for.

Mom had placed Luo Qingqing's trophy from the English competition at an ostensible spot at home. Grandma went over and studied it for a long while. Luo Qingqing would have preferred that Mom didn't do it, but Mom insisted on looking at it every day. Mom once said to Luo Qingqing: "Mom owes you. On the day of the competition, we couldn't even get anyone to cheer you on." Luo Qingqing was devastated at that moment, and her distress over the grievance Mom hid inside her outweighed the disappointment at having no one for celebration.

She remembered that back when she had got into the school affiliated with the foreign language university, Mom just cooked a couple of dishes to celebrate for her. But for Luo Qingqing, that had been heart-warming enough.

It hadn't been easy getting into the foreign language school. Since the junior high school entrance exams were cancelled, the enrollment of every good school had been subjected to donations and connections. Luo Qingqing didn't rank particularly high academically, so she had wanted to get in touch with Dad without anyone knowing and to at least ask whether he knew someone who could guarantee her acceptance. She swore to herself again and again that once she got into the foreign language school, she would perpetuate her luck, bid farewell to her blues and focus on her studies.

Good thing that she eventually got in. She hadn't sought help from Dad but barely managed to get in. As it turned out, she hadn't worried for nothing. She was the last student to be accepted on the merit of scores alone, but her student number preceded that of more than a dozen others, which was against logic. Her acceptance was pure luck and people might even suspect that strings had been pulled for her. So her seven years' high school had been motivated by the desire to distance herself from those who had indeed benefited from strings pulled.

Grandma touched the trophy gingerly and said to Luo Qingqing: "Grandma had wanted to come, but couldn't walk that far ... Qingqing you won't blame Grandma, will you?" Luo Qingqing smiled and shook her head.

Competition was no big deal, nor was university, because they lost all significance the instant she knelt down on New Year's Eve. Whatever her accomplishments during the year, however likely things were to look up, once her knees touched the floor that day, all happiness and aspiration were obliterated. All Auntie could do was to repeatedly boast about the DVD at home and about how good her cousin's English was, because only they could play undubbed foreign movies at home a long time ago, but ... it's no longer a big deal nowadays.

Only time was fair to everyone.

Luo Qingqing didn't envy that family and didn't care what happened to it. Its glory or humiliation, rags or riches, happiness or desolation, none of it could elicit from her the slightest interest.

Luo Qingqing used to go to Auntie's place a lot, in order to use the Internet for audio resources or to read original English magazines. She couldn't afford these at home but she wanted them. She was young then and couldn't understand all of the mean things that were said, so putting up with them hadn't been as hard as it was now. Even though she still remembered some of them and would play them back from time to time over the years.

She remembered hearing it from Auntie that Mom was pregnant with someone else when she was younger. The lover abandoned her in the end and she was kicked out by Grandma. Dad paid for Mom's abortion and ended up marrying her. When Auntie was recounting this, there was a look on her face that Luo Qingqing could never read. Thinking back, Luo Qingqing couldn't help feeling frightened, even today. Her parents had just divorced and she was still in primary school. How could she have known about abandonment or abortion? On her way home that day, Luo Qingqing walked too close to a bicycle more than once and she still remembered the raw pain of brushing her arm against the bicycles. When she got home, she dared not even look into Mom's eyes, because she didn't know what abandonment was, or abortion, and that scared her. Luo Qingqing had never mentioned to Mom any of these, and all she wanted now was to protect Mom.

Luo Qingqing remembered that the time she spent at Auntie's place became more and more unbearable. Auntie and Uncle who wasn't home a lot would often say things, for no apparent reason, to upset her. Everything at their place upset Luo Qingqing, even though in retrospect, Auntie wasn't having a good time herself. Auntie was always telling her how fun Europe was and how ignorant the foreigners were, but everyone knew that since Uncle struck rich, Auntie and her cousin had never stepped outside Shanghai. They hadn't even been to Suzhou, let alone Europe. But Luo Qingqing believed that her cousin would leave one day, since money was all one needed to go anywhere in the world nowadays. Maybe one day, her cousin would be better at a foreign tongue than she was, and would effortlessly skip all the efforts she had had to put in.

But if her cousin really left, what else would Auntie have to cheer for after boasting about it?

Mom finished setting the table, but Grandma had no smile and just stared at the table in a daze. Luo Qingqing was saddened at the sight of a busy Mom, and felt that Grandma's heart wasn't with them no matter how hard Mom and she tried. Mom seemed to have sensed Grandma's glumness too, so she took off her apron and asked: "Mom, are you ok?"

"I am ok, sit down and eat. Too many dishes for me," Grandma forced a smile.

"They are for all of us, come on and eat." Mom served Grandma the sour cabbage she had cooked especially for her.

But in retrospect, everything had some kind of reason to it. She and her cousin were born in quick succession. Auntie was in poor health, so it's natural for her not to take care of anything. From pregnancy to wedding, Grandma was with Auntie and her cousin was raised by Grandma single-handedly.

Luo Qingqing learnt later that after she left yesterday, Auntie told Grandma that she and Uncle intended to check into a nursing home when their time came, which implied that they wouldn't take care of Grandma. Grandma was deeply distressed over it.

Mom reassured Grandma over and over that she would take care of Grandma and live with her. But Grandma wouldn't stop sobbing. Luo Qingqing had dwindling faith that New Year was a happy time. For her, no tears would have been good enough. But the truth was that Grandma, Mom and she had all had the urge to cry, one after another. And they had the urge not because they were moved, but because they experienced endless pain.

"She doesn't even come for New Year's Eve now, and doesn't invite me to her place. I don't care, I will go anyway, Junjun will want me to go." Grandma muttered to herself stubbornly, and Luo Qingqing and Mom could only stare at each other.

The phone rang. Luo Qingqing picked it up only to be greeted by a tongue-lashing: "Qingqing I am telling you, go tell your auntie not to bother me with anything to do with your family anymore. Your grandma can live with whoever she wants and give her place to whoever she wants, why bother me with it, what business is it of mine!"

Dad's voice. This was the second time he had taken it out on her for being bothered by Auntie. She didn't know what to do about being blamed for something that wasn't her fault. Seeing how Mom was still trying hard to console Grandma, she turned back her head calmly.

Fine.

She gave a curt reply over the phone. Dad had become more surly over recent years. He had never talked to her like that in earlier times, and it crushed Luo Qingqing more than she had thought possible.

Dad hung up immediately. Luo Qingqing regained her composure and returned to the table. She debated whether to still go to Auntie's place. Auntie wanted her to go, but why had she contacted Dad then and encroached upon something she held dearest?

I am not going, Luo Qingqing decided. Why bother.

When Grandma was leaving, Luo Qingqing watched her unsteady steps and felt bad for her. Embarrassed, Mom was cleaning up the dishes that would last them a whole week.

Mom looked like she had a lot on her mind, and there wasn't even a hint of a smile on her face, the excitement of the morning gone without a trace. Luo Qingqing understood Mom's grievance, but didn't know how to comfort her. Luo Qingqing had a sudden flashback of the slap Grandma had once given Mom. Faced with Grandma's deep-rooted strictness after so many years, Mom again looked like a misbehaved child who had no idea where she was. Mom finally came out of the kitchen, her hands bright red from washing in cold water.

Mom said: "Qingqing, do you know, before the New Year Grandma and I went to the housing office to ask about living together. But your grandpa didn't change the names on the deeds before he passed away, so your auntie has to sign off for any moving, and your grandpa's workplace will need to sign too. After so many years, the workplace is nonexistent ..." Mom's eyes glistened and Luo Qingqing felt helpless.

Why did Grandpa have to die ...

Luo Qingqing kept the irrelevant thought to herself.

"Your grandma is in her seventies already. She was with me the whole day and tried her best. She would have liked us to take care of her, but I have failed her. It's all my fault that she is living by herself now. But Grandma has her own struggles, and I know that you have your grievance, but ... Grandma is attached to both sides and can't take any more pressure." Mom used the mop to wipe the same spot mechanically. And she eventually gave in to her tears, heart-wrenching tears. Luo Qingqing was overcome by tears, too, and words failed her which she could do nothing about. At that moment, she realized how badly Mom was hurting and how helpless she felt when she saw Grandma. She also realized that Mom had given her best for this family and one couldn't and shouldn't ask her for more.

Luo Qingqing went up to Mom and gently caressed her quivering back. It pained her to see the grey hair at the top of Mom's head. She turned her own head only to see her trophy at that ostensible spot looking on objectively at the silence, the grief and the sorrow, so condescending, so indifferent and so out of it all.

Before turning in for the night, Mom reminded Luo Qingqing that Dad seemed to owe them two months' child support. It was unclear whether Mom tried to make light of it when she mentioned it. It was a sensitive issue for both Mom and her, but not forgotten. But for Luo Qingqing, the reminder itself was poignant, whatever the disguise. She needed to see Dad. The torture of this afternoon opened her eyes to the insignificance of her own trivial emotions. She couldn't do much for this family, so her grievance amounted to little.

This was the last year. After this year, Dad no longer had to give her money. Her eighteenth birthday had seemed so distant, and now it was just a discolored contract keeping vigil over the sobering memories of growing up. Turning eighteen didn't take long, and it could have been the long-awaited relief for her, for Dad and for Mom.

Luo Qingqing and Dad were to meet in front of a restaurant. From afar, she saw a familiar figure leaning against a white sports car and blowing smoke into the air.

Did he buy a car?

Luo Qingqing found it ridiculous that he had claimed to be broke.

As she approached, Luo Qingqing noticed that Dad looked more energetic, hair waxed shiny. His belt was on bold display and his jacket could hardly cover his upper torso. The sun reflected off the GUCCI lettering on the belt, like an exaggerated focusing of light in a cartoon.

Was he out of his mind?

The more Luo Qingqing thought about it, the more hilarious she felt. The only real thing about Dad was the view of his back. Was she dreaming?

She was about to call "Dad" when she heard the greeting "Qingqing" and jerked her head around to see Dad walking towards her from the side, which startled her. She looked towards the GUCCI guy who turned his head at the same time to reveal a strange face.

"So you are Qingqing? You have grown up so much, can't recognize you anymore." The GUCCI guy stamped out his cigarette butt and said dramatically.

"Your uncle. You should have met him when you were young. We were eating just now."

"Dad," Luo Qingqing managed to call in a steady voice which turned out to be more difficult than before. She studied furtively the two men in front of her and tried desperately to find resemblance between them. She couldn't find any and that scared her.

After the greetings, the uncle took off in his sports car, and Dad and she finally settled down. Luo Qingqing looked for an opener to ask Dad for the child support he seemed to have forgotten, which was hardly enough for the living expenses of a twelfth grader. But if she went back home empty-handed, she would feel guilty towards Mom.

"Dad, I got into the foreign language university without having to take the entrance exams." Luo Qingqing said slowly, cradling the steamy tea cup.

"Right, I heard." Dad lit a cigarette, finally a gesture resembling that of the GUCCI guy.

"Oh, Auntie told you?"

"Yeah. I saw her husband a couple of days ago, too. At People's Square. He caught up with me on his bicycle and we had a drink." Dad didn't sound as enraged as he had over the phone, which put Luo Qingqing at ease.

"I haven't seen him for many years. Is he bankrupt now, what with the bicycle? It takes at least one hour to ride from his place to People's Square."

Dad didn't reply and just dragged on his cigarette.

"You should cut down on the smoke." Luo Qingqing looked at his *Zhonghua* cigarette pack and paused. "Even fancy cigarettes are bad for health."

"I got them at work for free, so why not smoke?" Dad said curtly. He was still so straightforward, sparing nothing.

"The uncle just now ... he looks really like you." Luo Qingqing stared at Dad breathlessly.

"Wouldn't that have been nice. He is loaded, as fate would have it, even though we came from the same parents." Dad gave a smile of either jealousy or grievance, Luo Qingqing couldn't tell.

But Dad had something there. Luo Qingqing had no illusion about it, especially the way the New Year was turning out.

"This uncle doesn't look that loaded. The ultra rich ride bicycles and wear rags, and weigh at home the rice they have bought to make sure they haven't been shortchanged." Luo Qingqing laughed as she realized she was going off track and couldn't find her way back.

"What do you mean, weighing their rice?" Dad extinguished his cigarette. They seemed to have hit the first topic they could converse on.

"Oh, it's nothing. He always weighs again the rice Auntie buys at home, as if he has all the time in the world."

"That's how you strike rich, you know. Some day the rice will weigh heavier than when you bought it." Dad was clearly implying something, and Luo Qingqing heaved a gentle sigh.

"What did you talk about when you had the drink with him?"

"Nothing, and none of my business. It bugs me when people come to me with things that have nothing to do with me." Dad put out his cigarette with practiced moves. And he looked both aggrieved and lost.

"I haven't been bothering you, have I?" Luo Qingqing smiled faintly, as she grabbed onto a topic that seemed more important than child support and Auntie's family.

"Getting into high school, getting into college ... I never had you spend unnecessary money for me, or pull any strings, or suck up to anyone ... right?"

The deli platter Luo Qingqing had ordered arrived, and she thanked the server in a low voice.

"Why are you eating this? Didn't you hate it when you were young?" Dad asked.

"I started liking it a long time ago ..." Luo Qingqing feigned nonchalance.

Dad lit another cigarette. He hadn't answered her question, so maybe any heart-to-heart dialogue between them was doomed from the very beginning.

"Dad, I have always wanted to ask you, if I hadn't got into any college and were good for nothing, you probably would have wanted me to marry myself off early so as to make it easier for you, right?"

"Ha ha ha ha," Dad laughed out loud. Luo Qingqing bent her head to work on a piece of duck and found that she didn't like the taste much. She tried very hard to pretend to listen.

"Of course. But the truth is I don't think much of the foreign language university. Why didn't you try Peking University?" Out of the blue, Dad popped a question that had never crossed Luo Qingqing's mind, and he was all seriousness.

"How could I have got in? You really think I am that smart?" Luo Qingqing put down her chopsticks and had a sudden thought. "Actually ... there isn't much difference between the scores required. Ten thousand yuan for each point of the score, would you have been willing to pay?" Luo Qingqing stared at Dad and asked solemnly.

"That's the going rate now? I know little about exams, but ... girls don't need to excel academically, no point."

"Ha ha," Luo Qingqing packed up her aggressiveness of a moment ago. Maybe aggressiveness wasn't her thing after all.

"Dad, I was awarded some money at the competition this time, so I bought you a shaver. I couldn't afford a fancy one, you know, since I ... don't have a lot of money." Luo Qingqing took a box out of her bag.

"You shouldn't have spent money, not when you are still going to school." But Luo Qingqing sensed that Dad had no real intention of blaming her.

Dad opened the box and saw the round-shaped shaver inside. He paused before putting the box in the pocket of his overcoat without a word.

Another long pause.
Silence.

"How is your mom?" Dad asked in a low voice.

"So so. She is still thrifty. I am in twelfth grade now and have a lot of expenses." Luo Qingqing tried to engage Dad's eyes, but he concentrated on smoking, which was a letdown for Luo Qingqing. "But Grandma isn't too happy. Before the New Year, they tried to get a place together, but it needed Auntie's signature." Luo Qingqing kept her eyes fixed on the pocket of Dad's overcoat and wondered why he had kept silent without even a "Thank you". Mom was the one who told her that Dad preferred round-shaped shavers. Had he changed his preference?

A pity that Luo Qingqing didn't really like the deli platter, the smell of which drove her more than once to put down her chopsticks as soon as she picked them up. Maybe only men had it in them to change so thoroughly without a trace of what had been before. Like Uncle, like Dad.


"Actually if it goes to court, you can still get three quarters. Grandma's portion can be given to you as long as she agrees to a will." Dad said slowly and without showing any emotional involvement, but he sounded sincere.

Goes to court?

Luo Qingqing never imagined family members going to court against each other, which she had only seen on TV. She didn't like Auntie but had no intention of taking her to court, and she didn't think Mom would do it anyway …

"Actually, I don't care what they are up to. Grandma is pretty pathetic." Luo Qingqing tried to brush it off.

"Your auntie can be totally discounted, remember this, you heard it from me. I don't want to say anything else, except that don't tell me anything about your family anymore. I told both your auntie and uncle that I am not going to interfere for any side, including you and your mom. It has been almost ten years, so why involve me. But if it had been before, I would have kicked his ass, how could I have been drinking with him!"

"Oh." Luo Qingqing picked at her rice and drank some soup. She couldn't think of anything to say and had no idea what not to say. She wanted to tell Dad things from the bottom of her heart, but Dad didn't want to be bothered, so what could she do?

When it's time to leave the restaurant, Luo Qingqing still hadn't mentioned the child support. She recalled that when she was in junior high and went to ask for money from Dad, Dad studied the bills one page after another, and every time his fingers flipped the pages, Luo Qingqing's heart would skip a beat. She was already eighteen, so probably she shouldn't ask anymore, nor did she want to anymore.

At eighteen, you should have the right to not want, to not do anything you didn't want to and to not want anything you didn't want ... That's the wish she had made on New Year's Eve. She had spent the whole night arguing with Mom, but the kowtowing the next day obliterated everything she had wished for.

She had hoped that Dad would hand her a couple of hundreds before she left, for the New Year if nothing else. That way she would have something to bring home instead of having to bite her tongue in the face of Mom's distant look.

But no. Dad waited with her for the bus. The bus took a long time to come and Dad never showed any intention of giving her money. Luo Qingqing's heart kept getting colder. But almost immediately, she got used to it and figured it must be the weather and not any disappointment. She had even started to think about how to explain her empty-handedness to Mom. She couldn't think of anything, but couldn't think about anything else.

"Qingqing, do you have money for the bus?" Luo Qingqing heard hope at that moment and her heart instantly warmed up.

She remained mute, neither nodding nor shaking her head.

"You silly girl, why didn't you say so?" Dad unzipped his bag to reveal a little bit of everything including newspaper ads, several packs of cigarette and a nail clipper.

"Hmm, I should have change." He stuffed all those newspaper, cigarettes, lighter and bus tickets into Luo Qingqing's hands. Head bent, he kept rummaging and the white steam out of his nostrils looked hurried.

Luo Qingqing saw his grey hair which reminded her of Mom's grey hair, but she could see no connection between the two.

"I remember having change. Just wait." He zipped and unzipped the bag, and his reddish palm slid in and out of each flat pocket in the bag. He shook the bag a couple of times only to hear keys.

Dad smiled apologetically. Luo Qingqing had never seen him so apologetic or smile in such a way.

She saw the shaky bus approaching from the distance. The street looked desolate, and colors were stripped from along the street as if infected by the decrepit bus. Luo Qingqing thought there was something wrong with her eyes as they were so dry as to hurt, which turned everything in her view drab.

Dad said: "I did get some change from buying breakfast this morning. That's ok. I will give you a ten. Ask the ticket collector for change, she will do it." Dad took a wad of money from the pocket of his overcoat and peeled off a ten for Luo Qingqing.

His overcoat was bulging with the box Luo Qingqing had given him.

Luo Qingqing took the ten nimbly and stepped onto the bus. She didn't say bye, because she was afraid that her nimbleness would be gone if she did say it.

Her commuter card beeped, the ten from Dad in her hand. Through the window, she saw Dad zipping up his bag, and his back was very hunched. For the first time ever, Luo Qingqing felt that Dad had aged. But even at his age, they still couldn't say what they really wanted to say to each other and could only ignore each other. Would it be like this for the rest of their lives? Love had long gone, and hate was becoming irrelevant, too.

She was just extremely distressed at that moment. She hadn't felt like this for a long time and found the feeling strange. But she had no room for tears, since it's New Year.

That was on the third day of the New Year, which Luo Qingqing would never forget. Because on that way, she became disillusioned about a lot of things. She blamed no one, and her having no one to blame made it all the more devastating. From the moment she mistook another person for Dad, she realized that she had really grown up and that so many years had gone by just like that. And she could choose either to remember or to forget.

That day Mom didn't ask her about the two months' child support, which wasn't exactly a relief for Luo Qingqing. As soon as she set foot at home, she felt like owing Mom, and once she stepped out, she felt like owing both sides. She oscillated among all those feelings of owing someone and couldn't find her place. She had no plan for the fourth day of the New Year but didn't go out, because all her schoolmates were studying for exams. And by this day next year, everyone would have been done with exams, but who would understand her "want" and "not want", her progress and regress, or her sorrow and disappointment.

"I let you do whatever you want today, and you are not going out. You hang around at home aimlessly. What are you thinking?" Mom poked Luo Qingqing's feet with her floor mop, so she had to raise her feet to mid-air. She swung them to the left when Mom mopped to the left and to the right when Mom mopped to the right. When she eventually couldn't stand it anymore and wanted to get up, Mom moved on with her mopping without having noticed anything. Mom never raised her head, and Luo Qingqing was left with her feet dangling and nowhere to put them down.

Auntie called at night inviting her over for wanton the next day in her customary excitable voice. She probably didn't recall the tears and wrinkled money of the other day. All she said was that she wanted vegetable wanton as a change from so many days of seafood and meat, and that she would like Luo Qingqing to join.

Luo Qingqing answered hesitantly, bogged down by too many thoughts.

She seemed to be sympathizing with someone who took undisguised pity on her, and seemed to be compromising for the sake of something other than family ties.

The firecrackers on the night of the fourth day of the New Year were deafening. Unthwarted, they disrupted the peace in every household every year. Luo Qingqing couldn't fall asleep, because Auntie's money was on her mind. She had no explanation for why she had taken the three hundred yuan that day, or why she had taken the ten from Dad. She found herself truly pathetic and ridiculous. She hadn't expected her compromise to legitimize others' condescension. She thought about kneeling down on New Year's Eve and about everything that happened afterwards, and realized she was so spineless. She thought about the bloodless Grandpa, the aging Grandma, the crying Mom and the silent Dad. They had all longed for each other and disappointed each other. Nobody had spoiled anybody, and their mere existence was embarrassment, hopelessness and torture.

The New Year's holiday was almost gone, and she was extremely reluctant to go to Auntie's place. She had no desire for Auntie to understand that she had failed to accomplish anything she wanted this entire holiday. The only thing she could decide for her two feet was to go or not to go. She knew that Auntie was in a difficult situation, but wasn't she too? And who could really carry some of the load for her?

The firecrackers lighting up one after another seemed to be shattering the heart, and Luo Qingqing couldn't hold back anymore amidst all the noises. She took refuge in the bathroom and dialed Auntie's place. After hearing a faint Hello from Auntie, she shouted: "I don't want to come, I really don't want to come, I don't want to come at all!" Thundering noises enveloped her again at that moment, and she couldn't hear herself or any reply over the phone.

I don't want to come! I really don't want to come! I don't want to come at all!

Luo Qingqing screamed at the top of her voice, tears rolling down her face. The bright colors of the fireworks were reflected off the spotted window of the bathroom, and crackling sounds assaulted her ears. She screamed again and again and still couldn't stop even after the line went dead on the other end. The climax of the fireworks this year lasted especially long, maybe because too many people had made it, or too many people wanted to make it, or too many people realized they could forget themselves after they had made it, or too many people realized that after they had made it, to do more of the same was the only effective aspiration in this world.

Luo Qingqing screamed till she was spent. Her tears were blown dry by icy wind creeping in from under the door to check on her. Mom was sound asleep in the next room. She could block out the noises, maybe because she had more important things on her mind. Those were the things that ruled Luo Qingqing's life and that she couldn't extract herself from or find fault with.

She was astonished to find that she was kneeling, at the moment she lost her voice. The astonishment far outweighed her fear. She had no idea what she was praying for, or whether her heart-wrenching screams could be taken for sincerity.

It was said that the old year was gone in the sounds of the firecrackers. But at the departure of the old year, who had aged, who had lost the way, who had compromised and who had matured?

Luo Qingqing felt exhausted. She stood up and pushed open the bathroom door.

She saw Mom in the dark.

She hadn't woken her up, which was good.

She wouldn't have wanted to disturb her. It's New Year.

# AFTERWORD
## The Texture of Time

I didn't truly appreciate the essence of novels till I was twenty-five. Before that, starting with high school, I had written and published hundreds of thousands of words in all kinds of writing. I made up a lot of stories, then I acquired some knowledge. It is only recently that I have started to learn and explore how to connect stories with knowledge.

For that, I am in the debt of many people, including my advisor Professor Wang Xingfu from the Department of Philosophy at Fudan University, and several mentors for writing from the Department of Chinese Language and Literature at the same university. Without their help, I might not have set out to think about my writing, about other people's fate, about cities' fate and about the mysterious connection between one fate and another.

Starting 2008, I wrote a series of novels in which the Workers' New Apartment Complexes were the backdrop. They made up the first half of this collection. The complexes were the Shanghai in my eyes and the only Shanghai I had experienced.

In the early 1990s, Acheng wrote in a collection: "After 1949, cities in mainland China started to be countrified, which was especially true for Shanghai. The entire exterior of Shanghai was frozen in 1949, like in a movie, and the city was gradually eroded into a big township. I look at Shanghai as if looking at a dinosaur's skeleton. New buildings keep springing up over the years which is eerie, as if new bone spurs were growing out of the fossilized skeleton. By the look of it, the new spurs will take over Shanghai." When he was writing this, I was growing up among the spurs at the edge of the city, and I did witness my hometown being taken over by the spurs. Such a mutation lasted through my adolescence.

Of course I can't sit around and admire my own works, thinking how special I am. I can only faithfully reproduce the appearance of the city from my memory and the subtle ethics of people in the city. But perception alone isn't enough. By learning about the time and space of where I am, I have started to learn about my own origin and history, and about how my own living space is different from others'. I look for myself and my country in a secular space. I see myself sometimes as an adolescent girl from the old apartment complexes, sometimes as a child from an incomplete family, and sometimes as the other half in a marriage. This is a searching process, experiencing process and cleansing process that is not exempt from pain.

Guanguan has a poem that I like a lot. It has spirit and depth and leaves room for thinking. Maybe the writing process I am trying to truly feel now is such a process:

*Lotus*
Mud was in the lakes before
And you remember the miles of lotus flowers
Swamps have taken their place
Only to be replaced by building after building
Buildings? You ask yourself
No, you see only roomfuls of lotus flowers.

September, 2012, Taipei

# Stories by Contemporary Writers from Shanghai

The Little Restaurant
Wang Anyi

A Pair of Jade Frogs
Ye Xin

Forty Roses
Sun Yong

Goodby, Xu Hu!
Zhao Changtian

Vicissitudes of Life
Wang Xiaoying

The Elephant
Chen Cun

Folk Song
Li Xiao

The Messenger's Letter
Sun Ganlu

Ah, Blue Bird
Lu Xing'er

His One and Only
Wang Xiaoyu

When a Baby Is Born
Cheng Naishan

Dissipation
Tang Ying

Paradise on Earth
Zhu Lin

The Most Beautiful
Face in the World
Xue Shu

Beautiful Days
Teng Xiaolan

Between Confidantes
Chen Danyan

She She
Zou Zou

There Is No If
Su De

Calling Back the Spirit
of the Dead
Peng Ruigao

White Michelia
Pan Xiangli

Platinum Passport
Zhu Xiaolin

Game Point
Xiao Bai

Memory and Oblivion
Wang Zhousheng

Labyrinth of the Past
Zhang Yiwei